LANDFALL

CHRISTOPHER DEON GATTIS

Writer
Book Publishing
Services

Copyright © 2019 by Christopher Deon Gattis
All rights reserved

No part of this book may be reproduced or transmitted in any form or by any means without written permission of the author.

Published with Assistance from
Writer Book Publishing Services
www.writerbookpublishing.com

Printed and bound in the
United States of America

ISBN: 9781096571414

Landfall: A Novel
By Christopher Deon Gattis

ABOUT THE AUTHOR
CHRISTOPHER DEON GATTIS

Chris Gattis writes books to inspire people to improve their lives through their faith, self-discipline, knowing your purpose and using "good common sense."

He has an Associate Degree in Christian Counseling from International Christian School and Seminary and is currently working on his bachelor's degree. In addition he is graduate of Best University Barber School in Greensboro, North Carolina and keeps his skills up to par barbering to thousands of inmates behind bars.

His Christian faith has kept him strong during the darkest moments of his incarceration. He has dedicated his life to helping others "right their wrongs" through a positive mental attitude.

He is the father of three "most beautiful children."

YOUR PURCHASE MAKES A DIFFERENCE

Editor's Note: Author Chris Gattis is giving a portion of each <u>Landfall</u> book sale to the International Christian College and Seminary. The following information was provided by the college, which each seeks to change lives and lower the recidivism rates of inmates.

International Christian College and Seminary (ICCS)

About: International Christian College and Seminary (ICCS) was founded in 2007 out of a desire to provide quality Christian education, with reasonable tuition. We currently serve over 600 inmates. We are approved through the Department of Education and accredited through the International Theological Accountability Association (ITAA). Valuing the Word of God and His knowledge as the cornerstone of wisdom, we strive to provide economical education alternatives based on Biblical principles in a Christ-centered environment. We are committed to equipping the saints to spread the knowledge of Jesus Christ throughout the earth. We prepare laborers in the fields of education through low-cost, focused instruction, ensuring a quality education for all students regardless of socio-economic status.

In researching other Bible Colleges that typically serve the needs of inmates, we found that most of them require payment in advance. For most prisoners, these payments are virtually unattainable. As a result, those who desire to continue their education are halted due to their inability to afford the exorbitant tuition. Our desire is to meet the inmates where they are in their time of need. As a result, we offer moderately priced alternatives to education which are feasible for our students. ICCS charges $9,497.00 for each degree, from Associate's through Doctoral, but we offer inmates an 85% scholarship which brings their total tuition to $1,425.00. In addition, we offer payment options of $5.95 down and $12.95/month with no interest and no collections. Students may also receive an additional 30% discount for pre-payment bringing their total tuition to $997.00. As you can see, we offer a significant reduction to our students who are currently detained. Our structured fee plan enables them to pursue their educational and spiritual goals and desires without having to worry about finances.

You may be wondering if receiving an education while serving a prison sentence is worth the effort in the end. Our research has shown recidivism rates are inversely proportional to a released prisoner's level of education. Emery University conducted a study and found the following:

- Ex-offenders who complete some high school courses have recidivism rates around 55%;
- Vocational training cut recidivism to 30%;
- An associate degree drops the rate to 13.7%;
- A bachelor's degree reduces it to 5.6%; and
- A master's degree eliminates recidivism completely with a rate of 0%.

Perhaps the best statistic isn't a statistic at all, but a person. Dr. William A. Sassman, RFC, M. Div., Ph.D., is a recent graduate of our program. He was an inmate at the time he began our program and, with the help of our ministry, succeeded in his endeavors to complete his education. He has also authored a book and credits his accomplishments to the hand of God in his life. Since completing our program, he has joined our team and is currently a Professor of Church Administration at ICCS.

Our goal is not just to educate those who have a thirst for knowledge; our goal is to show them how to receive the gift of the Holy Spirit and cleanse themselves of all sin. This, and this alone, is what gives them the strength they need to leave their sinful nature behind and begin anew. 2 Corinthians 5:17 tells us that "Therefore if any man be in Christ, he is a new creature: old things are passed away; behold, all things are become new."

Please refer to the following resources for additional information:

- Please watch: http://iccscampus.org/programs-for-the-incarcerated/
- For more information on ICCS please visit the following websites:
    - International Christian College and Seminary (ICCS): http://www.iccscampus.org
    - For more detailed information you may view our profile on the Central Florida Foundation website at http://cffound.guidestar.org/NonprofitProfile.aspx?OrgId=1142489&preview=True

ACKNOWLEDGEMENTS

No book of mine comes together without me giving thanks to my Lord and Savior Jesus Christ for putting the right people in my path to get the job done. A special thank you to Susan Cabe, my friend, mentor and sister in Christ for the countless hours she invested in typing, editing, correcting and retyping my manuscripts. There are no words to express my thankfulness for fulfilling my dream to see my second book in print. God bless you!

Also a special thank you to Michelle Owens at Writer Book Publishing Services for your invaluable input toward making my book a bona fide "must read."

Also I would like to thank my greatest supporters Karl and Jeanie Neuschaefer, Ken Walker, Bob Zippay, Charles Chandler, Iris and Dirk Apt, Janette Florence, Tosha Mebane, Tracy Sleigh, Billy Fearington, Billy Gattis, Liz Bigelow, Sandra Allen, Tonia Carter, Martha and Romeo Ferguson, Pamela Jones, Rosa Dixon, Satonna Evans, the Alphin Family, the Graham Family, Tiffany, Nicole, Brenda, Don Logan and Chaplain Hackett.

Without your prayers, visits, financial support and encouragement through letters and phone calls I would never have been able to live out my dream. I thank God for putting each of you in my life.

Also to Gail Cousin. I am so grateful for your beautiful presence in my life. You are such an inspiration to me and I love you for helping me through some of my darkest days. Thank you for your support. (Latoyia, Asia, Ashley, Roc and Morgan thank you for your many prayers. God Bless!)

A special thanks to my son Tyrick and my daughters Karizma and Chanaghauh. Because of your love and support, there's nothing I can't accomplish.

To all my brothers and sisters, nieces and nephews: thank you for your encouraging words and prayers during the years of my incarceration.

A big thank you to the volunteers at Piedmont Correction for making a difference in my life and the lives of my fellow brothers behind bars.

Also, I would like to thank all the faith groups and brothers that helped me get through all the ups and downs of life.

Rest in peace to all the family I have lost along the way while I have been persuing my dream of becoming an author: Junior Dixon, Michael Dixon, Parthenia Daye, Curtis Dixon, Janeatte Galloway, Billy Gattis Sr., Brenda Gattis and Jamie Gattis. Miss you all. God Bless.

Sincerely,
Christopher Gattis

TABLE OF CONTENTS

ABOUT THE AUTHOR	I
YOUR PURCHASE MAKES A DIFFERENCE	III
ACKNOWLEDGEMENTS	VIII
PROLOGUE	1
INCREDIBLE TESTIMONY OR UNBELIEVABLE RESULTS	5
THE LETTER	19
COUNSELORS	28
GOODBYE	42
A NEW BEGINNING	55
CLOSE ENCOUNTERS OF THE GOD KIND	68
A FAMILY TRADITION	82
ONE MORE HURDLE	92
COLLEGE BOUND	101
COULD THIS BE?	120
A TIME FOR EVERYTHING	136
DRIVEN BY GREED	145
AN UNEXPECTED, UNDESERVED GIFT	159
TRUTH OR CONSEQUENCES	170
A DESPERATE PLEA	180
DON'T SPOIL MY DAY	189
FRIENDS IN HIGH PLACES	202
MY SECRET FEAR	211
IN THE LIKENESS OF MY FATHER	221
FINALLY	238
CAN YOU WITHSTAND THE STORM?	249
EPILOGUE	262

Prologue

One Saturday afternoon, a few months before mom died, I was helping her clean out the attic. We spent the majority of the afternoon sifting through the myriad of boxes that, in addition to their contents, had collected their fair share of dust bunnies and creepy cob webs. Mom was always a stickler for donating old clothes and other "gently" used items to the local Goodwill. She was a firm believer in blessing others and in the process ridding her home of the potential dry rot and God knows whatever other kind of vermin this junk, I mean stuff, could possibly attract.

In the process I even lucked out and ran across some souvenirs from my childhood that I wanted to keep for old time's sake, namely my G.I Joe collection and my first leather baseball glove that was given to me by my dad. When he gave it to me he told me that his father had given it to him and he was passing it on to me as part of the Blake family tradition. I took a good long whiff of the leather, letting the scent soak into my nostrils before I placed it in the box labeled "Ryan's things."

While we were going through some of the other "treasure" boxes, we came across one slap full of trophies and medals and certificates commemorating my dad's achievements as a high school football star. At the bottom of the box I saw an old newspaper clipping that had yellowed over the years. In big bold black letters I read, "Blake Out with Torn ACL Injury." I asked my mom if this had anything to do with the reason why dad had forfeited his college career as an athlete. She proceeded to give me a detailed explanation of how the unfortunate consequences of life have a way of dashing a young man's hopes and dreams. She told me that my dad was more or less considered "damaged goods" after that injury and a lot of the recruiters didn't want to take a chance on a player who may not fully recover. She explained to me how the letters from colleges stopped coming, the phone calls slowed down and recruiters basically lost interest in him. The only other choice my dad felt like he had after his high school graduation was to join the military. His hopes were to travel the world and learn a trade so that he would have some employable skills after he was discharged. After a 4 year stint as an M.P., and a year fighting in Afghanistan, he was discharged and took a job with the sherriff's department.

Wow, I thought. The things you learn cleaning out the attic. I never knew about any of this and I'm glad I found this tattered old newspaper article linking me to my dad's past. What a comeback story. I just hoped that I could live up to his example and expectations. I gently placed the article back in the box and sealed it shut with tape.

Mom reiterated that dad's desire, and her's too for that matter, was for me to not only meet the standards set by my dad, but to surpass them. She told me everyone makes their mark on society and my parents wanted more for me than they had the opportunity to experience. She gave me a wide grin and that cute little pinch on the nose she always gave me to show me how much she loved me. She encouraged me not to worry and told me that they would always be there for me to help me realize my dreams.

Well, we finished rummaging through the boxes and managed to salvage four boxes of clothes, toys and what-nots for the Goodwill. As we were getting the boxes closer to the staircase, I noticed an old antique clock with a cracked glass leaned up against the chimney. From the dust and cob webs you could tell that it had been there for quite some time. I walked over to it, picked it up and placed my ear against it, hoping that I would hear the sound of it ticking. Mom looked my way and told me to gently shake it a couple of times and it should start ticking. I shook the clock, being careful not to do it too hard. To my amazement I could hear the tic toc sound begin to beat in perfect rhythm as the second hand swept across the clock face. Mom explained to me that the clock had been Grandma Louise's and that she had kept it after her death as a piece of memorabilia.

I knew there had to be a story behind why my mom kept this particular clock all of these years. I remember seeing, and yes hearing, that clock ticking away as it was perched above the mantle over the fireplace at grandma's house. I could hear it all night long, through the silence of the night, tic-toc...tic-toc...tic-toc. Mom explained that Grandma believed that time is a precious commodity that we've all been given. You can weather through the worst of storms and time will still be with you. Also in life you can experience love and joy and "father time" will celebrate right alongside you. Time is a gift that will help you overcome your greatest challenges and will eventually heal all sorts of wounds. We have a choice in life. Time can either be your enemy and make you bitter, or your friend and make you better. It can make you a victim or the victor, it's up to you if you choose to let it help or hinder you. Mom was one smart woman.

Incredible Testimony or Unbelievable Results

"If a man begins with certainties, he shall end in doubts; but if he will be content to begin with doubts, he shall end with certainties."
--Francis Bacon

The defender saw me coming across the court and he raced toward the edge of the court to stop the pass. I reacted with a quickness that even surprised me. Breathing hard, and with every ounce of strength I could muster from within, I drew the ball back and dribbled it through another defender, powering it through the net just as the buzzer sounded.

This was the third game of the season for the "Razor Back's" of Jackson Middle School in Brunswick County, Virginia. Our team celebrated the win by converging on the court, giving one another high fives while singing our signature victory chant. Coach Andrews even gave us a brief pep talk before he dismissed us, something that always encouraged us, but at the same time managed to keep us humble.

I grabbed my gym bag and headed for the exit door only to be met by angry clouds and torrential rains. I took a quick glance outside to see if my father's car was in the parking lot and was immediately filled with disappointment. Once again, as so many other times since Mom died, he was a no-show. I threw my gym bag over my head to shield myself from the downpour and ran to take cover under the carport, waiting for the rains to subside. It would be a long four and a half mile walk home, one I had done more times than I could count in the past.

As I was standing there dealing with all the emotions of anger, frustration and rejection, Coach Andrews pulled up. Through a cracked window he asked, "You need a ride home Ryan?"

I hesitated at first to give him the obvious response because I was afraid my dad would be angry at me for accepting a ride from a stranger. Although Coach Andrews was no stranger to me, he was to my dad because he never took the time to show up for any of my games. And he never offered support to my team in any way, knowing full well how important it was considering he played football in high school.

I glanced up the road to my left and then to my right to see if there was any sign of my dad's patrol car. You see, my dad was John Blake, the Sherriff of Brunswick County. When I realized the coast was clear I gladly accepted the invitation and hopped in the passenger side.

"Thanks coach," I said.

"No problem Ryan, that rain's coming down pretty hard," he said as he turned his windshield wipers to high. He then drove away from the curb, monitoring his speed like an old lady trying to maneuver her way through a busy intersection.

"Ryan," Coach said, "you did great out there on the court today. Your teammates, myself included, were glad to have you back in rotation after…. you know, the accident with your mom and all."

"Yeah coach," I said, "I'm glad to be back and that I could contribute to our success. It feels good to be a part of the team again."

"Well Ryan, if you ever need someone to talk to or a shoulder to lean on, my door is always open."

"Thanks coach," I said. "Coming from you that means a lot."

I turned my head away in an effort to avoid any more questions from him. As I was watching the rain dance off the window, I could feel the barriers come up to protect myself from any further intrusions. Coach was about to cross the boundary I had so carefully constructed over the past few months in an effort to hide my pain. The constant agony I suffered at home through physical abuse and emotional neglect festered like an open sore on my soul. I felt like the only remedy was to apply the right medication and give it time to heal.

I wondered what form the remedy I so desperately needed would take. I had grown to accept all the black eyes, busted lips and bruised ego as the norm in my life. This was the way my father chose to vent his grief, guilt and anger. You see, six months ago my mother was tragically killed by a drunk driver. My dad's coping mechanism, after attempting to drown his sorrows in alcohol, was to take out his frustrations on me by beating the crap out of me. If only my father would have come to the realization that my mom's death was a freak accident that could have happened to any innocent driver on the road that morning. I felt like him coming to this realization was the hope of his deliverance from his inner pain and my deliverance from his displaced anger.

Days like today often conjured up such a mixed bag of emotions. I often wondered if my mom lingered and suffered, or if she just quietly slipped off into heaven when Mr. Roanoke's truck careened through a red light going 80 miles per hour, blindsiding her car. I may never know the answers to all of these nagging questions, but rather will have to learn to somehow trust the words of my Aunt Shirl. She is my father's older sister. In an effort to console me, she encouraged me with the fact that God had a special place in heaven for His children. That explanation hardly put a bandage on the nagging wound in my soul. Deep down, I still wanted revenge for Mr. Roanoke and also for all the suffering my dad had been causing me. They were both in a prison of sorts; Mr. Roanoke in the state penitentiary for the next 13 years and my dad was serving his sentence as an inmate in the prison of his own mind.

Still deep in thought, I continued to watch the raindrops beat against the window as Coach Andrews turned his car towards my street. So many contradictory thoughts were running through my mind all at once. Was I partially to blame for her accident or was it as unavoidable as I thought it was? You see, my mom was on her way to school that morning because of a disciplinary problem I had had with another student. This student had called my dad a coward and a bully for locking up his dad for a domestic altercation. I did my best to ignore him but he kept provoking me. As I was trying to walk away from him he pushed me from behind and I fell headfirst into a locker. That was it! I turned and punched him twice in the face...wham, bam! Two teachers intervened, grabbing us before escorting us both to the principal's office. We were suspended for two days and our parents were called to pick us up. My mom never made it.

  I guess my dad was also dealing with his own guilt issues. I would later find out the truth of this horrible avoidable accident from a newspaper article hidden away in a Bible on top of the fridge. The day before the accident my dad had pulled Mr. Roanoke over under the suspicion that he was operating a vehicle under the influence. The article also stated that my dad had admitted to investigators that he had even smelled alcohol on his breath, but failed to administer the breathalyzer. Dad had confided in me that Mr. Roanoke, like himself, was a veteran of the Afghan War. He always had a soft side when it came to veterans, especially those who had served in combat. He also had mixed feelings when it came to all the empty promises made to veterans by government officials. But as Sherriff of Brunswick County, he was also a representative of the government. The irony was that my dad felt like he was not appreciated for the sacrifices he made to preserve and protect what that government stood for. So consequently he let Mr. Roanoke off the hook and issued him a warning to get his tail light fixed. This decision would ultimately cost him everything he valued in life; his wife and his reputation as an outstanding sheriff with an impeccable record. Subsequently, he was put on administrative leave pending a full investigation.

I remember the sick feeling I had in the pit of my stomach when I realized I was being blamed for something that really wasn't my fault at all, even though there was a certain amount of guilt I still harbored. And I didn't know if it was my dad's guilty conscience or the alcohol that fueled the anger that he ultimately took out on me. Either way it was no excuse to beat someone who you supposedly loved and who was totally dependent on you for their protection.

I also believed part of my father's will to live died the day he was called to respond to my mom's accident. He had no idea that he would find the love of his life crushed behind the wheel of her car. In essence I lost both of my parents that day, my mom who died a tragic, senseless death, and my dad, who died a different kind of death, one of guilt.

I snapped out of my "brood moment" of thoughts, dreams and what-ifs when coach tapped me on the shoulder.

"Ryan, we're here," he said with a kind of distraught look on his face.

I guess the fact that I spent most of the ride gazing out of the window into the rain in silence had him concerned.

"Are you okay?" he asked.

"Yeah, I'm fine. I was just in deep thought about some things," I replied.

"Well son, I'm going to extend my offer to you again. If you ever need someone to talk to, my office door is always open," he said reassuringly.

"I'll be fine, just working through some stuff. See you tomorrow at practice. Thanks again for the ride," I said as I got out of the car.

I jogged up the walkway to the house trying as best I could to dodge the raindrops. I came through the front door to a house that at one time was clean and inviting and often filled with the smell of freshly-baked cookies. It now resembled a war zone in more ways than one. There were always huge piles of dirty dishes in the kitchen and mounds of dirty clothes in the laundry room to greet me. And instead of the sweet smell of home baked cookies, the house always reeked of stale onions. Dad liked to eat raw onions when he drank. I'm not sure if he liked the taste of them, which is hard to believe, or if he was trying to cover up the stench of the liquor. Anyway, I hated this new "survival mode" dad and I found ourselves in without Mom in our lives.

I even thought about running away one time, but I'm knew my dad would put out an A.P.B. to the surrounding law enforcement agencies. Another time, I thought about buying a bus ticket to my Aunt Shirl's home in Wilmington, North

Carolina. I wondered if someone would be suspicious of a 13-year-old riding on a bus unaccompanied by an adult and call the authorities. But deep down I would have to admit the real reason I stayed was because I loved my dad and needed him. The physical and emotional abuse were very much a present reality, but prior to Mom's death this man was my hero and my protector. He taught me so many things; how to ride a bike, how to swim, how to hunt and fish and even how to cook a great steak on the grill. He had even attended some of my games when I played "Pee Wee Mite" baseball. It made me feel so special to realize that he was proud of me at one time.

I never would have imagined that the man I so admired and looked up to would turn into such a monster. And he had changed so suddenly. I knew life had a way of throwing curve balls at you. I was just struggling to know who the pitcher was -- God, or Satan?

The circumstances I was wrestling with brought a Sunday school lesson to my mind. It was about a character in the Bible named Job. God had allowed Satan to test this man to see just exactly what he was made of. Job lost everything that defined him, including his reputation. The only thing that Satan left intact and unscathed in Job's life was his relationship with God. He certainly had a lot of questions for God, and so did I. So many whys. Why did all of this have to happen to my perfect world? Why did the mother I needed so much have to be taken from me? Why was I being used as a punching bag as a way for my dad to vent all of his issues? Hopefully one day God would reveal the answers to me for all of these whys.

I took off my soggy shoes and socks and headed straight for the bathroom. A hot shower was just what I needed to take the chill off my scrawny five foot eight, 125 pound frame. After my shower I slipped into a pair of shorts and a tee shirt. I headed for the kitchen to fix a snack. I never knew what would be in the fridge. I would have liked to have had a ham and cheese sandwich, but no such luck. Once again dad didn't remember to do the grocery shopping, so I had to settle for a P.B. and J. sandwich with a glass of milk.

I gobbled down the sandwich, grabbed my journal and headed for the couch to relax for a while before dad came home. I had found that one of the ways to cope with all of the trauma was to write in the journal mom gave me for Christmas a couple of years ago. She too had journaled during her growing pains and thought it would be beneficial for me to write down my inner most thoughts as I was beginning my journey into adolescence. Dad thought it was "corny" for a boy to write down his feelings. He thought it would have been more manly to talk to him, but this journal with all the entries of what went on behind closed doors would later prove to be priceless to me.

I also wrote about all the things that occupy a young male teenager's mind; sports, girls and one day growing up to be a professional basketball player. I jotted down a few notes about the game, highlighting my stats before closing it and turning off the TV. It wasn't too long before I dozed off to sleep and escaped into the world of my dreams. I found myself dancing with Princess Miller, a girl in my math class that I had a crush on. She had the cutest dimples and freckles all over her face. In my dream, we were dancing to a love song, standing toe to toe and gazing into one another's eyes. Just when I leaned forward to kiss her I was rudely awakened by the sound of someone fumbling with their keys at the side door to the kitchen. This incessant rattling could only mean one thing; my father was once again drunk and disorientated and struggling to unlock the door. I had grown used to these annoyances; smashing trash cans, fumbling keys and the like. In fact, they were quite typical of his usual drunken antics. Unable to successfully maneuver his key to unlock the door he began pounding his fist against the metal frame while simultaneously shouting, "Open this door before I kick it down!"

I barely had a chance to respond when I heard, "Open the door you piece of..." Before he could start with his obscenities, I unlatched the lock and opened the door.

"What took you so long?" he shouted.

He screamed at me, this time pounding his chest with his fist and bobbing back and forth, "I pay all the bills around here, buy all the groceries and I can't even get into my own home!"

At that moment I knew it would be in my best interest if I stayed away from my father. He was in one of his drunken rages, and there was no logic to how he responded to whatever crossed his path. Anything that I said or did at that point could trigger a violent reaction.

"Answer me boy!" my father demanded.

"Dad, I was asleep on the couch," I said frantically.

"Sleep, sleep, that's all you do around here while I'm working and paying the bills."

Before he gave me a chance to reply, he grabbed a glass off of the counter and threw it against the wall, shattering it to pieces. I was so terrified that I ran to my room and shut the door behind me. I was hoping that he would calm down and leave me alone. I was more than relieved when heard his footsteps in the hallway bypassing my room as he headed to his bedroom.

It didn't take long before my father came staggering back down the hall, punching his fist on my door, demanding that I open my locked door. I could feel the terror in the pit of my stomach, anticipating the inevitable. Within a matter of seconds he kicked down the door, shattering the wooden frame. There he stood, six feet three inches and 270 pounds of pure muscle with a look of unexplainable, insane fury in his eyes. He lunged toward me and the vicious assault began. Blow after excruciating blow to my head and back. My only defense was to curl up into the fetal position in an effort to shield my head and stomach from the brutal punches. I couldn't retaliate. I was totally helpless and hoped that he would wear himself out and stop from sheer exhaustion. For a full agonizing 60 seconds I was this man's punching bag. I had in essence become his scapegoat, the one on whom he projected all his pain, frustration and the unrelenting agony he so desperately tried to anesthetize with alcohol.

I cried out with a loud voice, "Dad please stop you're hurting me."

I kept repeating this over and over. After what seemed an eternity the beating ceased. What I had experienced can only be compared to the carnage left in the wake of the winds of a violent hurricane -- sudden, vicious and deadly.

As he exited my room I could hear his footsteps heading down the hall to the kitchen. He would always take a drink after he beat me. I don't know if it helped to ease his sense of guilt, or if it acted as a catalyst to fuel his anger. All I know is that there was a welcome calm, a peaceful interlude, not unlike the peace experienced when the eye of a hurricane passes over. But, just as with a hurricane, the most violent and destructive winds occur after the eye has passed and the backside of the hurricane strikes. As unimaginable as it may seem, my father came back into my room. This man resembled nothing less than a monster. His eyes were bloodshot red and full of rage. He possessed the same demeanor as a wild animal stalking his prey. He then methodically continued to unleash a second round of assaults on me. The pain, the fear, and yes, the anger I was going through at that moment defied description.

He had hit me in the past, but he never came back to "finish me off." I just laid there on the bed, crouching in terror, hoping that Mom's angel would appear and rescue me from this savage beating that no one deserved. But those thoughts never came to fruition. My father grabbed me by the leg and yanked me off the bed like I was a rag doll in the mouth of a wild animal, shaking its prey to death.

"Dad stop you're hurting me," I cried out in tears.

"I'm gonna teach you to respect me in my own house," he said with a slur. "When I get through with you you're gonna wish you never caused me this pain."

"Dad please stop you're scaring me," I blurted out as I kicked and squirmed, hoping he would let go of my leg.

He said nothing else, but with deliberate, calculated premeditation proceeded to take his belt off and beat me uncontrollably on every part of my body. I screamed and yelled, desperate for him to stop this vicious, senseless assault. By this time my body was a symphony of pain. Every part of me ached, and the lashes of his thick leather belt stung like fire. I could see blood on my clothes, but I wasn't sure where the lacerations were. I had never been so terrified, so traumatized and so utterly helpless in all my life.

I finally managed to break free and ran into my father's bedroom and grabbed the gun he kept in his nightstand. By this time he had staggered down the hall and was standing right in front of me in the doorway with that same look of unexplainable rage in his eyes. As I raised the gun in his direction, my hand shaking as nervously as a rattler on a rattlesnake, I said "Dad please don't make me do this, I'm tired of you hurting me."

My father kept coming towards me, his hand raised, grasping his belt, poised for the next round of attacks. I closed my eyes and squeezed the trigger as hard as I could. The gun discharged a single, fatal bullet hitting my dad squarely in the chest. He fell to his knees and then his whole body went limp as he hit the floor.

"No.... No.... No..." I screamed out. "Dad, why did you make me shoot you?" I yelled. He said nothing as he laid there in a pool of his own blood; his eyes fixed, gazing at the ceiling as though he had seen a ghost.

THE LETTER

"To send a letter is a good way to go somewhere without moving anything but your heart."
-- Phyllis Theroux

It was midnight and I couldn't sleep, tossing and turning on the "iron board" jokingly referred to as a bed, hoping to find a comfortable spot to rest my weary body. Sleep would be my only escape from my surroundings; gray dingy walls, the paint peeling from the constant humidity, thick plastic windows weathered and stained, long overdue for replacement, and the smell, oh that unforgettable smell. Kind of musty, kind of funky....it was a cross between dirty socks and the lingering aroma from whatever our last meal was.

Sleep was also an escape from the inner turmoil of thoughts, fears and yes, from the nagging guilt. Now, to add to the barrage of anguish in my soul, I was perplexed and confused over a letter I had received earlier that week from my Aunt Shirl. For whatever reason, she was reaching out to me and asking me to come live with her pending my upcoming release from Camp Penitude for juveniles. You see, for the past four years, eleven months and seven days, this "rehabilitation institution" had been my home.

I had come here when I was just 13 years old, young, disillusioned and very scared. This was my sentence, my debt to society, the consequences I must bear for the crime of killing my own father in cold blood. I had never felt more alone in my life, even though I was constantly surrounded by other internees, guards, and reformatory employees. It's an aloneness that can't be explained, only experienced. It's a feeling that only those who have been estranged from their families for years can understand. In all the time I had spent there, not one letter, visit, or any communication from a family member, none whatsoever. So I thought a lot about that letter from Aunt Shirl, and wondered if maybe it might have been her way of dealing with her own guilt issues.

The only piece of property I had to remind me of my past was a photo of Mom and me snuggled up in the bed as she read a book to me. My dad took the picture with a new camera he had gotten for Father's Day that year. He wasn't much of a photographer and consequently got frustrated if the pictures would turn out blurry. Mom blamed it on lack of use and the fact that dust had collected inside the lens as it sat on the shelf of the bookcase in his office. If I didn't have this photo in my wallet when they arrested me, I would have been shopping in my mind for a picture of Mom and me for years.

Since I couldn't sleep, I reached my hand under my mattress and retrieved the letter Aunt Shirl had written three days ago. I had read it over several times already. It was really still kind of surreal to me, the fact that someone, blood kin no less, remembered me and reached out to me. This was the first inclination in years that anyone, other than a few of my friends in the camp and some of the staff members, cared about me at all.

For someone incarcerated, whether in a juvenile detention center or a maximum security prison, to receive letters from a friend or a loved one who has an interest in them is absolutely huge! Usually those "make me smile letters" are saved and read over and over during your sentence as a reminder of the connection you have with those who are on the outside. It gives a prisoner hope during those times of loneliness and discouragement that can become particularly unbearable on sleepless nights like this.

I opened the envelope and took out the letter. The faint scent of the bakery she owned still lingered on it. With that vague sweet smell came many memories -- memories of happy summer visits on the coast, frolicking at the beach, and memories of helping Aunt Shirl in her bakery. Memories of belonging, of feeling safe and loved.

My mind drifted back to a time when my life was as picture perfect as any other teenaged kid from the suburbs. Prior to my mother's death, life at 112 Daye St. was pretty good. My parents got along fairly well in spite of their busy work schedules. They both managed to set aside time to "woo" each other with lunch dates, walks in the park, and even a periodic family vacation to Wilmington, NC. This is where my Aunt Shirl and her family lived. She was the coolest person you'd ever want to meet. I was always pampered by Aunt Shirl, seeing I was my parents' only child. She would usually buy me whatever I wanted. One Christmas she bought me my favorite childhood toy – a shiny red electric mini truck. It had pin stripes down the side and was loaded with all kinds of accessories -- all the bells and whistles that any eight-year-old boy could get completely occupied with. Playing with that truck put me in another world. I would find myself "joy honking" my horn at everything that crossed my path. More often than not it was my cousin Terrance, Shirl's son, riding his bike around in circles yelling, "Catch me if you can!" Terrance's younger sister Tonia would be chasing me around in her pink play jeep, bobbing her head from side to side listening to tunes on her handheld CD player.

Her letter read:

Dear Nephew:

There is absolutely no excuse for me not picking up a pen and writing to you in these past five years. I've been working around the shop, filling orders, and time has just slipped by. I just want you to know that you have been on my mind and in my prayers. I was notified by the courts that you will be released from the detention facility in a couple of weeks. I feel like the least I can do at this point in your life is to extend an invitation for you to come live with me; that is of course assuming you will accept. I've prayed about this and feel the Lord leading me to give you something no one else in your life has been willing to give you...a chance. My door is open to you until you can get established and figure out the direction you want your life to take. I know this is short notice, and like I said, I have no excuse for not being there for you all these years.

Call me when you get this letter and let me know if you will accept this offer so Terrance and I can pick you up.

Looking forward to hearing from you.

Love,
Aunt Shirl

P.S. Enclosed is $100.00 to help you with canteen items. I don't know if you have a Bible, or if you ever read it. Please read over these verses when you can. They speak directly to your situation. "He gives power to the weak, and to those who have no might He increases strength. Even the youths shall faint and be weary, and the young men shall utterly fall, but those who wait on the Lord shall renew their strength, they shall mount up with wings like eagles, they shall run and not be weary, they shall walk and not faint." (Isaiah 40:29-31 NKJV)

After reading the letter for the fourth time I neatly folded it up, carefully placed it back into the envelope and then stashed it back under my mattress. Somehow it seemed the scent of fresh bread stayed in the air, though. I sighed.

Aunt Shirl was deeply rooted in her Christian faith. Every time our family visited her home on the coast of North Carolina, we undoubtedly would find ourselves in church on Sunday mornings. Those occasional annual visits to church were the only time I can recall being in church as a child. Aunt Shirl played the piano and sang. I loved watching her play and hearing that raspy voice belt out classic Southern Gospel hymns. She had no need for a microphone; that voice would carry from one end of the church to another. I remember thinking to myself one Sunday morning as I listened to her sing, "I bet God and the angels can hear this clear on the other side of glory!" The words of those old Gospel hymns told me about how truly precious we are to God and how He will be with us through every storm, every battle and every misunderstanding. Sometimes I would find myself singing some of those words to myself as a saying to me that no matter how discouraged I felt, or how bleak the circumstances appeared, I still had hope that one thing remained constant. God's presence.

As I pondered on the words to these songs, the Bible verses in Isaiah, and the invitation extended to me for a place to start my life over again, a peace came over me. It was as though the Lord was telling me "Be still and know that I am God." (Psalm 46:10 NKJV) Trusting in the confidence of those words, I drifted off into a sweet, restful sleep.

The next morning, as with every other morning, I was awakened by the sound of guards yelling, "Get out of your bunks and stand in line, it's count time!" No matter what time you fall asleep in prison, it's always "rise and shine" at 6:00 am for the morning count. This is standard operating procedure for most prisons and juvenile detention centers to insure all inmates are accounted for.

"Just two more weeks of this awful screaming and yelling," I thought to myself as the guard walked past me and asked for my identification number, checking my name off of the daily roster sheet.

After the count had cleared I washed my face and brushed my teeth before the morning breakfast was called. I had quite a busy day in front of me, a pleasant break from the monotonous routine of a life without choices, at least the ones that govern a person's physical existence.

I did believe something. One choice that no institution can take away from you is the choice to be free on the inside. Free from the boredom, free from the hopelessness, and free from the shame. Free to hope.

I can't say that I understood why I felt like there was hope for me, there was just a knowing that somehow, someway, my life would one day have meaning and purpose. I once heard someone say that God uses people to accomplish His plan on the earth. Maybe He was using Aunt Shirl to provide a refuge, a safe haven where I could get my bearings and start a new chapter in my life.

That morning I was scheduled to see the dentist at 8:00 am and I also had a 9:30 appointment with Dr. Grimes. She had been my psychiatric social worker for the past four years. She was appointed by the state to work with prisoners and to evaluate whether they were suffering from a mental health disorder or not. Once she arrived at a diagnosis, treatment in the form of therapy was recommended and medications were sometimes prescribed.

I still had some unresolved anger issues and battled depression periodically. Whether or not these were actual mental health disorders, or if they were a consequence of the environment I came from or the environment I was presently a part of, I wasn't sure.

Anyone who kills another human being, be it in self-defense or otherwise, will inevitably have issues to deal with.

Dr. Grimes knew all the details surrounding my case and recommended psycho-therapy treatment. Basically what that boiled down to was that we would talk about my past and I how chose to allow it to affect my present and my future. There was no changing what happened, but I could change the way I chose respond to it. It was painful at times talking about my mom's death, the abuse, and the murder, but Dr. Grimes helped me sift through my emotions, come to terms with what had happened and how I, at 13, had reacted. I really didn't feel as though I had a choice. Since I was a minor when I committed the crime, it seemed to persuade the judge to show me favor when considering the mitigating circumstances of my case. So now, I was nearing the end of my five year sentence for voluntary manslaughter.

Looking back to when I first came to Camp Penitude, I was extremely physically and emotionally traumatized, not only by what I had done, but by what I had suffered at the hands of my father, the very person in this life who should have taken care of me. Dr. Grimes had taught me that in psychology, this type of emotional trauma is referred to as a "father wound." It's a term that describes a child's emotional response to a father who was either absent, dysfunctional or abusive. In one of our sessions, Dr. Grimes told me that we are all created with a need to be affirmed by our fathers. I asked her what that meant and she said, "We all desire the acknowledgement of our fathers. It's such an integral part of our identity that it literally defines our very existence."

It helped me understand the utter hopelessness I was experiencing at that time. Dr. Grimes brought me to the realization that the one who was supposed to validate my life as a son had forfeited that relationship through violence. And the real tragedy is, that out of fear for my own life, I killed the one who should have protected me, affirmed me and been an example to me.

COUNSELORS

"People start to heal the moment they feel heard."
--Cheryl Richardson

I just made it to my 8:00 am dentist's appointment. All went well. It was just a semiannual cleaning and checkup. I had some time to kill before my next appointment at 9:30 with Dr. Grimes, so I slipped back to the dorm and retrieved Aunt Shirl's letter. I wanted to get Dr. Grimes' opinion, not only about what she had written, but possibly why. I was still juggling a lot of mixed emotions and needed someone who was detached from the situation, at least emotionally, to give me their perspective of Aunt Shirl's intentions.

It was a beautiful day, sunny and warm. You could hear the birds singing and the faint sound of traffic in the distance. Camp Penitude is located on the outskirts of Brunswick County, Virginia and the summer heat can be quite oppressive, to say the least. It was early April so we still had another month or so of pleasant weather, just right for taking a walk and clearing your head.

As I walked along the sidewalk, I continued to reflect on my past, on the series of events and the choices I had made that had gotten me to where I was that day. I was 18 years old and by all legal standards a man. I felt like all I had managed to accomplish in the past five years was to get my GED. There was so much that I had missed out on, things I would never get back...high school, proms, graduation. I often wondered what my classmates at Jackson Middle School and Coach Andrews thought of me. Where was the help he had once so generously offered me? Another regret was churning around in my mind. I never did get to ask my middle school crush "Princess Miller" out for a date. I started walking more quickly. Man, I needed to stop this "soul train" of self-pity or I was going to have a wreck!

I shifted gears and began to think about my trial. That was the last significant event that to determine my destiny, at least the one I had lived for the last 60 months. I can remember my lawyer spending countless hours with me trying to explain to me the seriousness of the charges against me. A 13-year-old who commits murder in the state of Virginia, can, under certain circumstances, be tried as an adult. I was too young at the time to realize how the cards were stacked up against me. I was going to court facing charges of murdering my own father, a law enforcement officer, and all that with no more than an underpaid, overworked public defender to try my case.

I can remember feeling numb, numb to the pain, numb to the consequences, numb to everything. I just sat there and stared off into space. I could hear the words, but had no inclination of the gravity of what this man said to me. Later on I had to admit, even though this man was a court-appointed public defender, he did his best to see that I received a fair trial and spared me a much stiffer sentence.

Killing a officer of the law, one who served in a small tight knit community, regardless of the circumstances, was always a more challenging case for a defense attorney. After my lawyer engaged in a series of negotiations with the district attorney, along with providing expert testimony, I was offered a plea bargain. If I plead guilty to voluntary manslaughter my sentence would be five years in juvenile detention.

What helped with my case was that journal I had kept. In it, I had documented all the episodes of verbal and physical abuse, right up to the day that I shot and killed my father. I had no idea that one day it would be used in a court of law to help exonerate me from first-degree murder charges. I explicitly remembered the judge reading over the pages of my journal, shaking his head in disbelief. Something struck the heart of the judge that day when he read my accounts of how, time after time, I was abused and beaten. He even realized that I often feared for my own life. Even though my dad was a well-respected lawman in that town, that reputation was shattered in the eyes of that judge when he saw what this man was like behind closed doors. I was relieved to know that finally someone knew the truth, even if that truth was somewhat distorted by my crime.

Nobody wins in this case, neither the defendant, the plaintiff nor the lawyers. Two people's lives' were forever altered the day I shot my father; Sherriff John Blake died a tragic physical death, and his son Ryan Blake died an insidious emotional death. So to put me away for five years meant nothing more to me at the time than if you had dug a grave and covered me over with dirt.

I made my way around the admin building to the side entrance. Dr. Grimes' office was just down the hall to the left. As I approached the open door to her office, I noticed that she was speaking with someone. It was none other than the notorious Mrs. Brown, affectionately referred to by the inmates as "the brown recluse." She was a state-appointed social worker with the bedside manner of a poisonous spider. Everyone cringed when they knew they had an appointment with her. "Talking to her is like talking to that wall," said one of my friends once, and he was right. She acted like she was just there for a paycheck, with no real concern for our welfare or our rehabilitation.

As I took a seat on the wooden bench in the hallway and waited for them to finish discussing their caseloads, I grasped Aunt Shirl's letter, staining it with the sweat that had built up on my hand. I was so nervous, with so many thoughts darting in and out of my mind, so many fears smothering me and unanswered questions haunting me. I wondered. I wondered if Aunt Shirl took me in -- how would the other family members receive me? I killed one of their own. Would I have to watch my back like I've had to in prison?

It had taken me a while to confide in Dr. Grimes. For some reason I supposed that all government employees were my enemies, if for no other reason than the way my father had treated me. I knew that wasn't a logical deduction, but that was how my immature mind rationalized how to deal with people.

When I first met her, she reminded me of a school teacher, her sandy hair pulled tightly back in a ponytail. Stylish black-rimmed glasses graced her face, highlighted by a faint hint of blush on her cheekbone. She wore no wedding ring on her finger, so I assumed she wasn't married.

When she first introduced herself to me, she told me that she had been working with juveniles for 20 years. She convinced me that she would do everything in her power and within the limits of her professional ability, as dictated by state jurisdiction, to help me as much as she could.

On the wall behind her desk was a collection of photos of young men and women neatly tucked in wooden frames. On a previous visit I had asked her about the photos. She told me the stories of these young people who she felt had miraculously intersected with her life. It was obvious how much she cared about these young men and women who she had helped to overcome mental health disorders. Most, if not all of them, came through the system dealing with tremendous challenges so much greater than the guilty verdicts of the crimes they had committed.

I recall an early conversation we had concerning some of these people. "Some of the young men and women I have counseled suffer from mental illnesses such as depression and personality disorders," Dr. Grimes said, "while others have been victimized at the hands of custodial adults, parents and caregivers, the ones who were supposed to care for their children. Some as young as eight years old were molested and raped, while others were physically and emotionally abused. The statistics are mind boggling! And we wonder why our young people are turning to alcohol and drugs in droves? It's a vicious circle. What medicates their pain winds up causing a far worse pain in the form of addiction. Now the victims of these heinous crimes become the perpetrators of greater crimes to support their habits. The greater crime is the one committed out of desperation, justified in their own minds by the victimization and the compulsion to feed an addiction that can never be satisfied. They invariably wind up behind bars, sick, broken and defeated, and ultimately sitting in front of my desk."

"And others, like the ones in the pictures you see, I was able to help through intensive therapy, wise counsel, and the greatest remedy of all, love. Over the years, I have intentionally displayed these pictures in a prominent place to be an inspiration to others. Other people like you, Ryan. Regardless of where we come from or what has happened to us, we have a choice to make. We can let it defeat us, or we can overcome, against all the odds, with the right treatment, a positive attitude and hard work."

It took several months for me to warm up to her, but as time progressed I learned to trust her enough to open up to her. It was extremely hard for me to make myself vulnerable to her in this way, especially in a prison. A part of you wants to trust, to be heard, and to be understood. Another part of you wants to recoil back into the safety of what's familiar, the self-isolation of your cell, a place where you can lick your emotional wounds in private. Some people were so traumatized that they pretended to be engaged, when all the while they were putting on an act, becoming the stars of their own show. They had done this all their lives. It was completely natural to them, so much that they were not even sure they knew the truth about who they really were.

Dr. Grimes was not only intelligent and professional, she really cared about our well-being. It doesn't take a rocket scientist to figure out whether someone genuinely cares about you or not. My mom once told me, "People aren't interested in how much you know until they know how much you care." She cared, and that meant more to me than all the diplomas hanging on her wall.

Over the five years I was incarcerated, and as I progressed in treatment, I started sharing with Dr. Grimes some of the details surrounding my case. Although she had read my 12-inch-thick case file, she still wanted to know how I was coping with the trauma of the abuse, the loss of my father and the challenges of institutional life. For a while I "clammed up" and told her I didn't want to discuss anything to do with my father...whatsoever. I buried those memories in the courtroom and I didn't want some woman I didn't even know digging them back up. Didn't she know what the horror and the stench of unearthing a rotting corpse of memories would be like, all so I could come to terms with the finality of death? Not me. I was fine in my masquerade of shallow feelings and managed responses...just going through the motions of life in "juvie."

When Dr. Grimes realized that we were not getting anywhere, she confided in me about her mother abandoning her as a child. Evidently her father was not in the picture at all, because she never mentioned him. For awhile, she was placed in a foster home and sexually abused by her foster dad and verbally abused by her foster mom. She told me that for years she lived under an umbrella of guilt and shame. These negative emotions escalated to feelings of rejection and eventually worthlessness.

She told me that often people in these situations get to the point that they lose hope; hope in themselves, hope in others, and yes, even hope in God. Dr. Grimes got to this point and tried to take her own life by overdosing on some over the counter pain medications. It was definitely a stroke of divine intervention that kept her from dying that day. You see, her foster mother wasn't even supposed to be home that time of day. She had come home early from work, plagued by the headaches she would often get after arguing with her foster daughter the night before. Her foster mother found the 15-year-old lying across the bed and unresponsive; an empty bottle of pills lay on the floor beside her. Some said that was fate that she survived, others said luck, and others said it was nothing short of a miracle. She never told me which she thought it was.

"What happened after you took the pills?" I inquired.

"Well, I'm glad you asked, Ryan." She continued to tell me that she was rushed to the hospital and the poison was pumped out of her stomach. Another five minutes and she would have lapsed into a comma. She told me that it was a very painful experience, in more ways than one. Once she was coherent enough to answer questions, the doctor of course wanted to know why a young, beautiful and intelligent girl like her would want to take her own life. She told him everything, about the sexual abuse and the constant verbal abuse. It was like tidal waves of bottled up anger and frustration were released. "I just sobbed," she said, "for myself, for the terrible shame I felt, and for not even being able to end this nightmare called my life."

She continued to tell me, "Child Protective Services were called in to investigate the matter. Without getting into all the details, I was taken out of that home and eventually adopted by a couple who wanted to add to their growing family of three girls and two boys. Another miracle, a teenage adoption! My adoptive parents were the ones who made it possible for me to go college and graduate and eventually pursue my dream of becoming a psychiatric social worker. I promised myself I would make a difference and use my education to help other young people who had been through the same horrible things that I had endured as a child."

"Well," she continued, "during my internship I worked alongside other doctors and social workers who studied mental health disorders and I became intrigued with the science. I was fascinated with the therapeutic techniques and the possibility of being able to help people, especially young people, deal with the stigma of mental health issues. As a result of my training I was offered a job with the state and requested that I be assigned to Camp Penitude. I found that when you discover your passion you make a connection with your deepest motivation. My motivation, my desire, is to help young people like you, Ryan, reach their full potential through self-analysis, individual counseling, and group therapy. It's crucial that you understand these concepts of introspection and confession if you're going to come to terms with the wounded part of your soul that so desperately needs to be healed."

The more sessions I had with Dr. Grimes, the more we connected on a deeper level and were able, together, to get to the root of what was plaguing my mind. It was very painful and sometimes I dreaded those visits...those long talks of exposing my inner fears and my anger. But the more I talked about it, the more I bounced these feelings off of her analytical, sympathetic mind, the more I was able to realize that even though I was helpless to stop what was happening to me, I could make a choice not to become a perpetual victim. She made me realize we've all been victimized in one way or another, even my dad. There had to be a reason he treated me like he did, beyond the excuse of having the drug of alcohol in his system. There was a part of me that loved that man and at times a part of me that hated him. Deep down I longed for the relationship that only he could give me, one I would never have.

Dr. Grimes made me realize I had to make a choice, to be free, free from everything that defined me up to that moment and free to become a man, a man with a purpose and a man with a destiny.

The greatest adventures in life start with the first step. Mine was a job in the camp kitchen washing dishes for 70 cents a day, six days a week. A little anti-climactic from pursuing your destiny to manhood, but I had to start somewhere. Dr. Grimes made a few phone calls and got me the job. I told her about my Aunt Shirl and her bakery and how I used to watch her make her unique creations of wonderful desserts for her loyal customers.

It wasn't much, $4.20 per week, but at least I was able to buy a few items from the canteen. The value of money takes on a whole new meaning in prison. That wasn't all I had to my name. Mom had set up a trust fund for me to go to college. Deep inside I wanted to achieve that goal, mainly because of what Dr. Grimes had accomplished with her life. At that point I wasn't sure what I wanted to study, I just knew that that dream had the potential to become a reality. Ironically my dad left me in his will, but I had to forfeit his estate because of the murder.

Dr. Grimes was finally about finished with the visitor in her office, the "ole brown recluse" herself. She just noticed me sitting on the bench in the hall and motioned to me with her hand that it would just be a few more minutes. Well good, it was already 9:35 and I wanted to spend as much time talking with her as I possibly could. Her office was one of my "escape pods," one of my respites from the drudgery of prison life.

Just then Ms. Brown walked past me to head back down the hall to her office. Was that a smile I detected on that old prune face? Yes, but no. I think it was; I thought I saw teeth, but maybe I was mistaken, maybe it was a "Fig Newton" of my imagination. To tell you the truth I didn't even know if that woman had any teeth at all. Nobody had ever seen her smile. Talk about miserable! Well, she did a good job of destroying the evidence. In no time flat, she whisked around, did a complete 180 and high tailed it down the hall. Her slick move reminded me of a pro ball player swirling through the air just before he slam dunks the ball. Next time maybe we can get that move of hers on film. People in here would pay some serious money to see that.

I was glad she was gone and I could finally get into Dr. Grimes' office. What a welcome relief. I felt safe there, a feeling I hadn't experienced since my mother died. On her desk, next to the picture of her adoptive parents were two Bible verses, one on either side of the picture. They read:

"For I will restore health to you and heal you of your wounds says the Lord, because they called you an outcast." (Jeremiah 30:17 NKJV)

"See then that you walk circumspectly, not as fools but as wise, redeeming the time because the days are evil." (Ephesians 5:15-16 NKJV)

As I was about to take a seat, I was greeted with a warm smile and an outstretched hand. "Good morning Ryan, how are you doing today?" she asked. It was always comforting being greeted that way, a great big smile, a warm handshake and a kind, graceful demeanor. You don't get that every day in prison.

"I'm fine," I said as I smiled back at her.

"Have a seat," she said. "Before we get started I need to tell you that we're going to have to cut our session a little short. My niece is graduating from college today, and I told her I would be at the ceremony. I promise to make it up to you next week, including the five minutes I was late starting our session. Fair enough?" she asked.

"That's fine, Dr. Grimes," I answered. I was anxious to begin. "I received a letter from my Aunt Shirl, my dad's older sister, three days ago. I would like for you to read it and give me your thoughts." I handed her the letter, sweat stains and all. It took her all of 30 seconds to read it. She smiled as she handed it back to me and said, "Great news Ryan, I'm excited for you. Have you made up your mind yet?"

"Nah," I said, "I wanted to get some feedback from you before I call her."

"What's the hesitation in your voice? I don't understand," she said with a furrowed brow and a look of concern.

"Well," I said, "my family used to take trips to see Aunt Shirl every summer. She lives on the coast in Wilmington, North Carolina. I have some wonderful memories of those visits. The last time I saw her, or heard anything from her for that matter, was five years ago at my sentencing hearing. She wouldn't even so much as look my way. As you well know, family members of the deceased are allowed to speak at these hearings to voice their grief. They're given an opportunity to vent their anger, respectably of course, or just address the defendant in some way before he is taken to prison. When asked by the judge if she had anything to say she just shook her head no, and then burst into tears. It's been four years, eleven months and eight days since I've heard anything from her. Can you see why I'm so hesitant to call her?"

"Well Ryan," Dr. Grimes said as she looked me in the eye, "I don't claim to have all the answers but you must understand she lost her brother and she was about to lose her nephew for five years. People react to tragedy and the loss of loved ones in different ways. The way you process grief may not be the same way she does. The fact that she contacted you and is offering you a place to stay until you figure out what direction your life will take speaks volumes. I believe she never stopped loving you, but in order for her to help you now she had to go through her own bereavement process. Does that make sense to you?" she asked.

"Not really," I said, "but I'm trusting you to be right since you have a lot more wisdom than I do."

GOODBYE

"If you're brave enough to say goodbye, life will reward you with a new hello."
-- Paulo Coehlo

Life at the infamous Camp Penitutde was finally coming to an end. Aunt Shirl was scheduled to pick me up around 9:00 the next morning. Since I had to be a parolee for nine months after my release, Dr. Grimes convinced me that living with Aunt Shirl would be the best way for me to avoid recidivism. I couldn't wait to exit the building and hear the sound of those obnoxious squeaking, squealing, sliding gates close behind me for the last time. I was about to embrace the world I had been so disconnected and alienated from for the past five years of my life. I was feeling so many different emotions simultaneously -- fear, joy, and yes, even a sense of sadness.

The sheer exuberance of being free again had overwhelmed me to the point that I decided to take a jog around the track, not only to get some fresh air, but to clear my mind from the barrage of thoughts knocking around inside my head. Usually when I was jogging I was daydreaming about those things I missed out on while in prison. I had often wondered what it would have been like to drive a car, have a girlfriend, go to college, find a job, live on my own; you know all the things young men like me want to experience.

As I rounded the curve at the top of the track I recalled a therapy session with Dr. Grimes where she told me that it was perfectly natural to desire these things. In fact, she would have thought it was quite abnormal if I didn't have these thoughts and aspirations of ownership, responsibility and prestige. She said these are the natural appetites of the soul, a pathway to the deeper values that would give me self-worth and purpose. Prison could, if you let it, take much more away from a man than his freedom. For those who fall victim to the insanity of prison life, the consequences are devastating. They are the ones who became "casualties" of the system, revolving-door inmates who just can't seem to make it on the outside.

I had been so young and impressionable when I came here. I'm not sure why, but somehow I was a little more resilient than most and as a result was able to absorb the effects of boredom, monotony, estrangement and the myriad of other dysfunctional aspects of institutional life. I was not without help though. I learned to trust those who were committed to my well-being, namely Dr. Grimes and a handful of guards and prison staff who had not surrendered their call of duty to the rampant corruption of prison life. And of course there was God. I was still working through a relationship with Him. I knew He was real and I prayed when things got really tight, but that was about the extent of it. Maybe my new life would change my understanding of who He was.

As I jogged, I couldn't help but think of my bunkmates that I would be leaving behind. Amidst all the chaos, violence and isolation, I still managed to develop some very meaningful friendships during my stint. There were five guys in particular who impacted life in a positive way.

One of them was my bunk mate named Eric, more affectionately known as the "whiner." He complained about everything you could imagine -- the sports shows that were on TV, the slow elevators, the lack of spices in the food, the temperature of the water in the shower, too much noise, you name it. The list went on and on. And because of his intellect, witty personality and his way with words, he also came to be known as our jailhouse lawyer. One time he submitted a grievance for the lack of adequate air circulation in our dormitory where the temperature averaged 80 degrees during the summer. Well, he won that grievance and we wound up with four rotating fans in every non-air-conditioned dorm and a cooler filled with ice water to boot. Pretty slick, huh? Just like any competent lawyer that you would want defending you, Eric was a good man to have on your side if you ever got into a bind or had a bone to pick with admin.

Another inmate who I thought of was Derrick Matthews, a.k.a. "D. Mac." We jokingly referred to him as our pharmaceutical rep. He was the one we could go to if we had a toothache, couldn't sleep or were suffering the frequent bouts of constipation that often plagued us due to eating too much processed food. He was the guy who knew all the homemade remedies to help a brother feel better. I remember one time I was having flu like symptoms -- sore throat, achy and running a fever. Just like on the outside, medical visits in prison didn't come without a price. It cost $5.00 to see the doctor, a pretty steep price to pay considering I only made $4.90 per week at my job in the kitchen. It would have cost me over a week's salary to pay for one visit. I was definitely "inmate poor" by convict standards so I paid a visit to the pharmacist. D. Mac whipped up a concoction of hot and spicy soups, two aspirin, and of all things a cup of hydrogen peroxide. When you're in prison you have to make do with what you have. Within 24 hours I was feeling better. Granted, I had to get under the covers and sweat it out, but this homemade remedy D. Mac brewed up from a recipe his grandpa taught him did the trick. My tab for this medication was five single cup coffees, a measly 60 cents. That was a deal that I couldn't pass up.

    Kevin was another guy that I had grown to respect over time. He was caught up in the gang culture that existed behind bars, and that fact alone commanded a certain amount of respect from others. Kev, as I called him, stood up for me one time when a gang was trying to lure me into committing acts that could escalate to violence if I refused to comply. When I first came to Camp Penitude I was very impressionable and very scared. My initial experience with gang members and their territory, referred to as "turf," came while I was standing in line at the canteen one day. A couple of guys tried to extort me out of some money. They told me that I owed them rent money for living in their dorm. That's funny, I thought to myself, the state owns this prison, so how could I owe you rent money? It was useless to try and offer these guys an explanation, so consequently one of them got in my face and said, "I'll see you back in the dorm." Even though I was afraid, I was determined to stand my ground. Kev happened to see the whole incident and walked right up to those guys and said, "He's with me, back off." I really didn't know Kev that well at the time -- I had only seen him at a couple of basketball tournaments we had played in. Since I didn't know him personally, and I didn't run with his crew, I was kind of shocked that he defended me like he did. All Kev said to me after the incident was that I owed him one. That payback would come in the form of playing on his basketball team. I might have been skinny, but I was tall and I was fast.

    My respect for Kev grew over the years we were incarcerated together. Although he never resigned himself from his gang membership, he was someone I could always count on to have my back; a great advantage considering how unpredictable the world of prison could be. Kev even signed up to complete his GED and graduated with honors; a great accomplishment for someone with the odds stacked so heavily against him.

    Another dude I met was Slone. He was definitely a horse of a different color. He was a rich kid who grew up in the suburbs, and was the "politician" of the guys I ran with. Every program that was made available to us, whether that was Alcohol Anonymous Assistance, Narcotics Anonymous, Men's Club, Outreach, you name it, he was the groups' president. I didn't know if it was because no one else showed interest, or because of his personality, but he was the man to stay in good with if you wanted to get active in your recovery. Administration took a liking to him because of his consistent involvement in leadership. It got to the point where some of the guys referred to him as a snitch because he was always in the programmer's office talking with one of the corrections officers. It was rumored around the dorm that if he didn't like you he had the pull to get you moved to another dorm. Not a good way to build trusting relationships, especially in a shark tank called prison.

Slone and I became friends when I signed up for the A.A.A. (Alcoholics Anonymous Assistance) class. Even though I wasn't an alcoholic I went to the classes to gain knowledge about the addiction. I wanted to gain some insight into why my dad made some of the choices he did. Why did he choose alcohol as a coping mechanism when he could have chosen counseling to cope with my mom's death? I may never know the answer to that question, but listening to Slone speak about the power of this drug and how it affects behavior helped me to cope with my own issues.

The bunk mate that I most closely identified with was Tank Evans Jr. His real name was Joseph, but since he stood six foot, five inches and weighed in at 280, he acquired the nickname Tank from his "bunkies." We not only were the same age, but we also shared a lot of the same interests. He loved to play basketball and rummy and he also taught me how to play chess, a game that I had always felt was reserved for rich, educated people. I grew to enjoy those long matches of strategy and concentration. They helped us keep our minds sharp and it somewhat alleviated the incessant boredom that plagued us day in and day out.

Tank and I developed a special relationship with each other because we shared similar stories. Even though the way we grew up was as different as night and day, the circumstances that got us to Camp Penitude were almost identical. He confided with me about his crime, which incidentally was the same as mine, involuntary manslaughter for killing his father.

He learned of my offense from a website called inmate.com. This website enables the general public access to information about anyone who is incarcerated. All you needed was a name and an OPUS number (Offender Population Unified System). It was common practice for inmates to have a friend or family member go to this website and find out what charges other prisoners were convicted of and how long their sentences were. Sometimes people in prison lied about the severity of their crimes and the length of their sentences. Well, all it took was a click of the mouse and a quick phone call to reveal the truth. Nothing was sacred anymore as long as there was internet access.

One day while Tank and I were in the yard taking a breather after four games of "B" ball, the conversation took a turn. He started to confide in me about the details surrounding the murder of his father. I could see the pain in his face as he rehearsed the details of that fateful day.

He said, "My dad was a great preacher and the Pastor of a growing congregation. Mom was right by his side, praying for the people, working in the children's ministry and encouraging my dad when he would get overwhelmed with juggling the responsibilities of leading a ministry and a family. Somehow my dad fell into the trap of an affair with a young woman at his church. I was so young at the time and I didn't know all the details -- just that this was going on for years before the truth ever surfaced. Well, my mother found out about his infidelity from a mutual friend of theirs who also attended the church. I was only 13 at the time and really didn't understand what she must have been going through. You know, all the anger, the betrayal and the fear."

"One afternoon when I came home from school they were arguing back and forth, hurling accusations at one another, screaming at the top of their lungs. I'd seen them argue before, but never anything like this. My mother was absolutely livid, and in a violent rage had confronted my dad about the affair. He reacted by grabbing her by the throat and throwing her to the floor. She was struggling to get free, kicking and squirming, trying to scream while he was choking the life out of her. All I could think of was that he was going to kill her if I didn't do something, and fast. I tried to pull him off of her, begging for him to stop, but I was no match for his strength. I went into the kitchen and grabbed a butcher knife and proceeded to stab my dad multiple times in the back. I didn't count the number of times I stabbed him but the coroner later said it was ten wounds. I was just as hysterical as they were and kept stabbing him until he went limp in a pool of his own blood."

"Wow," I thought, "Someone who committed practically the same crime I did and knows exactly what I'm going through."

"Do you ever think about your father?" Tank asked.

"Yes," I replied. "In spite of all the abuse and alcoholism, I'll always love him and I still miss him very much. He wasn't always that way. After my mother was killed by a drunk driver he lost his passion for life and he changed overnight. He became an angry, bitter man who took out his frustrations on the person who was closest to him...me. It took me a long time to come to terms with the fact that often circumstances in our lives occur that are beyond our control. Although we should take ownership for the way we choose to react, sometimes the situation is so desperate we don't feel as though we had any other choice but to take drastic action."

I paused for a moment and collected my thoughts. Looking him straight in the eye I continued, "You know, for years I was on this tremendous guilt trip that would have consumed me had there not been some professional intervention. Dr. Grimes helped me come to terms with all the negative emotions. She enabled me to overcome those destructive thought patterns. I've learned to forgive my father and myself and put the past behind me. I'm still a work in progress, but at least I have a firm foundation and I'm willing to take the risks to move toward complete wholeness."

I could tell by the look on his face that that last phrase puzzled him so I said, "Tank, I'm OK with me. I'm sorry for what happened and I can't change it. What I can change is the way I respond to my choices. I'm totally responsible for my decisions, whether they are made under extreme stress or not. I am choosing to go forward, forward in forgiveness, forward in faith, forward in freedom!"

I could tell that I had connected with Tank on a level that no one else had been able to. I suggested he fill out a requisition for an appointment with Dr. Grimes. I knew that she would be able to help him.

After my run, the yard closed and I spent the rest of the evening packing up what few belongings I had managed to accumulate over the past five years. I decided to give away my most prized possessions which consisted of a radio and headset and some toiletries to a few of the less fortunate guys. Some inmates really struggled and did without a lot of the "extras" that made life a little more bearable. The consequences of crime have a way of shattering relationships and burning bridges. Hence there was no one to send money for canteen items, no one to place phone calls to, and no one who took the time to write or visit. I jumped on the chance to relieve some of that pain and loneliness.

The next day couldn't arrive fast enough for me. I said my goodbyes to the fellas in my work area and thanked officer Shieldard for giving me a job even though I didn't have any experience. I was surprised with a going away present, a homemade pineapple cake; special order from the guys who worked with me. That was my favorite and they knew it. I really wasn't expecting anything and appreciated their thoughtfulness.

Considering how the head stewardess was always complaining about being over budget, this was quite the treat. Sometimes even "contraband" would go undetected and inconspicuously find its way into a cake or a pie or some other item that was not technically on the menu. Eric, my bunkmate, told me they were planning on doing something more, but a half pound of turkey had come up missing and Ms. Kelly, the kitchen Gestapo officer, a.k.a. head stewardess, was on a rampage trying to weed out the perpetrators.

Later that night when I got back to my pod, I sat down and wrote a letter to Dr. Grimes:

Dear Dr. Grimes:

When I first came to Camp Penitude five years ago my soul was in a deep, dark place. You were the one that gave me the help I needed to keep me from drowning in the overwhelming sorrow and the misery of being locked up. I have to admit, when I first met you, I thought you were like all the other prison doctors I had heard about. I figured you'd just prescribe enough medication to numb the pain and never deal with the underlying issues. But you were different.

You went past the "put a bandage on it" approach of treatment and reached out to me with compassion, a compassion that cared enough to treat the cause of the disease, not just the symptoms. Throughout the course of those therapy sessions I came to the realization that I was a very bitter and angry young man because of the abuse that I was subjected to. Those emotions were eating away at my soul, and I was dying a slow death, one that I felt like I deserved because of all the pain I had caused so many people. But I found hope in you, Dr. Grimes, and in the inescapable images of those faces of the young men and women in the pictures on the wall in your office. They were your success stories, the ones who you were able to help get past their pain and hopelessness and give them a new lease on life. I hope that my picture will one day be among those in your "Hall of Fame." The greatest lesson you taught me was that our lives are like a book with many chapters and full of ironies. The most puzzling one being the thing that is holding my soul captive may be the very thing that sets me free. The un-forgiveness I have harbored towards my dad and ultimately towards myself was more of a prison than the walls that were confining me to this juvenile facility. I was serving life without parole in the prison of my soul until you took the time to talk, to care, and to give me hope. I must admit I feel freer than I ever have because you believed in me, in your training, and in God. Because of the confidence you gave me, I was able to believe in myself as much as I can. I hope to one day help someone else come to that same understanding. I will end this letter with a sincere thank you from the bottom of my heart for giving me a sense of purpose that I never thought I could find.

Yours Truly,
Ryan

    I skipped breakfast the next morning. I was so filled with anxiety knowing that in less than one hour I could officially punch the clock and say, "time served!" I said all my goodbyes and slid the letter under Dr. Grimes' office door. As much as I would have liked to have thanked her personally, it may have been deemed "inappropriate" by some of the other state employees. They are very strict when it comes to any expression of emotional attachment, and that's understandable.

The officer in receiving issued me my civilian duds, a pair of outdated jeans and a washed-out, button-down denim shirt. The jeans were about three inches too big in the waist and were so long they dragged the floor and the shirt was so big it literally just "hung" on me. At least the shoes fit. They were mine. "Oh well, a small price to pay for freedom," I thought.

The officer handed me my release papers, resource pamphlet and a $45 gate check, compliments of the prison system's so-called rehabilitation program.

"Good luck," the receiving officer said as he extended his hand to shake mine. "I wish you much success outside of these walls, young man," he said with a smile.

"Thank you sir," I replied as I headed for the exit door and out to the gate of freedom.

Aunt Shirl and her son Terrance were waiting in her car, a light blue minivan. As the officer and I made the short walk to the gate, we were met by an unexpected gentle rain that seemed to come up out of nowhere. It felt so refreshing, such a blessing! The gate squealed open ever so slowly, the sound of rusty metal on metal accompanied by a loud beeping sound. Those noises may have sounded obnoxious to some, but it was like music to my ears! I walked through that gate a free man. I looked towards the heavens, closed my eyes and whispered, "Thank you Lord."

A New Beginning

"Every day is a new beginning; take a deep breath and start again."
-- Unknown

Cousin Terrance drove most of the way back to Wilmington. I just soaked in the symphony of sights, sounds and scents like a child experiencing the wonder of creation for the very first time. I was absolutely enthralled with the vibrant colors of the trees, the hip hop music coming from the radio, and even the faint smell of the exhaust coming from the barely cracked window. You know you've been liberated, or should I say resurrected, when you're enjoying the smell of exhaust fumes. I realize these are things that people take for granted, and in most cases probably wouldn't even give them a second thought. But when you've been "sensory deprived" in a predictable, monotonous environment for what seems like an eternity, anything out of the norm is like a miracle.

Aunt Shirl spent the first hour of our journey ranting and raving about how much I had grown. She turned her head and looked apprehensively at me sitting in the back seat and said, "The first thing we're going to do after you get settled in is take you shopping to get you some decent clothes. You're over six feet tall and as skinny as a rail. Did they even feed you in there?"

I know I must have looked like a lost orphan in that pitiful "going home" outfit they issued me. I can't say the outfit did anything for my ego, but considering all the attention that was being showered on me, accolades for my attire weren't really necessary at that point.

After a few hours of driving we stopped briefly at a drive-thru restaurant...another sensory explosion of sights, smells and tastes. As we continued the drive home and I was chomping down on the best chicken I'd eaten in years, Aunt Shirl proceeded to fill me in on the latest family news. She told me that her daughter Tonia was doing well at UNC Wilmington, pursuing a degree in business. Shirl also informed me that her sister, my Aunt Carrol Jean, was up to her usual antics of poking her nose in everyone's business.

I was only halfway paying attention to her. What I really wanted to do was to ask both Cousin Terrance and her why, in the five years that I had been incarcerated, had neither one of them bothered to write. Not one letter in all that time to see how I was doing. Now they show up with the "save the orphan" mentality. I can't say that I totally understood their motives, but I was nonetheless grateful for their help. This probably wasn't the right time to express my questions and concerns, but deep down I still felt like I deserved an explanation. I just smiled a halfhearted grin as Shirl continued with the latest updates on the family.

Just as we were pulling back out into the highway, a Department of Corrections transfer bus passed us heading west. Well, I thought to myself, I know where they're headed. Seeing that bus was like being awakened from a beautiful dream. It immediately brought so many unpleasant thoughts...the intimidation of being under constant surveillance and the loss of personal dignity that accompanies that suspicion that I had just left. I felt myself spiraling into a "death dive" of negativity when I consciously pulled the throttle stick of my mind and leveled off my thoughts. Oh, I could go on for eternity about the sick feeling that gripped my stomach, but I focused on being thankful. Thankful that during my stint I had been blessed with so many good friends and even more thankful that I was embarking on this new and wonderful experience called freedom.

Out of nowhere I heard Aunt Shirl say, "Wake up Ryan, we're home."

Without realizing it, I had drifted off to sleep the last couple of hours of the ride. I gathered the few belongings I had managed to accumulate in the past five years of my life and headed towards the house. Cousin Terrance had apparently had enough family time. He gave his mom a quick kiss on the cheek, gave me a tap on the hand, and headed in the opposite direction towards his car parked in the front of the house.

"I got other plans, get up with you later cuz," he said out of the window as he drove away.

The house had remained pretty much unchanged from what my childhood memories could recall. There was a fresh coat of blue paint on the outside and I could tell the roof had recently been replaced. It was such a pleasant sight. Neatly cut grass, hedges that were uniformly trimmed and rounded lined the front and sides of the house, all graced with beautiful multi-colored flowerbeds lining the perimeter.

Even though the house was about twice the size of my parents', the inside was just as warm and inviting as the outside. The furnishings reflected Aunt Shirl's taste, a little old-fashioned, a little cluttered, but it was definitely a place where you felt loved, accepted, and most of all, safe. I glanced around the living room looking for some of family photos of my parents and me, but they were no longer on the mantle above the fireplace. As I continued my way to the kitchen and reached for the fridge to get a cold drink, I realized the photo of me that was once on the door was also gone. I knew that I was no longer the cute little boy I was in years past, but I still wasn't quite sure what to make of that.

Anyway, what really caught my attention was when I went downstairs to the basement. Uncle Matt, Aunt Shirl's husband, had remodeled it into an entertainment room a couple of years before he died of lung cancer. It was like being in an amusement park for me. There was a pool table, a pinball machine and all kinds of electronic games that I had never laid my eyes on before. "Wow!" is all I could bring myself to say.

Although my memories of Uncle Matt were vague, the American flag that was draped on the back wall served as a reminder to us all for his patriotism. He, like my dad, had served his country in the military. I'm not sure of what branch, or even if he ever saw combat. That wasn't something people discussed much, at least the people in my family.

"Make yourself at home," I heard Aunt Shirl say, as I came back upstairs into the living room. I guess she missed the can of soda in my hands. "I'll be right back baby; can't hold water like I used to," she blurted out as she hurried off to the bathroom.

As she exited the bathroom, she was talking a mile a minute about all the things she needed to get done and all the places she needed to go. I decided it would be best to hold off on asking her what happened to the family photos.

"Ryan, your room is upstairs, first one on the right. I bought you some new sheets and pillow cases. And when you get yourself situated we'll go to the outlet store and do some shopping. I know that's not the best place to get a new wardrobe, but anything's better than what you've got on," she said.

Well, she was right. Even if I wasn't going to get designer clothing, at least something that fit right, even if it came from the local thrift store, would sure do more for me than what I was wearing.

When I did come downstairs Aunt Shirl was on the phone with her daughter, Tonia. She was a couple of years older than I was and we hadn't seen each other for years. I used to call her Buzzie because to me, as a little girl, she resembled a bumblebee with pigtails. My most vivid memories of her growing up were those bright yellow dresses Aunt Shirl would dress her up in, and if that wasn't enough, she would wear big yellow butterfly bows to match. Some of the things parents put their children through in the name of love.

"Here Ryan, Tonia wants to say hello," Aunt Shirl said as she passed the phone to me.

"Hey Cousin Ryan," Tonia said with excitement in her voice.

"Hi Cousin Tonia," I replied.

"How have you been doing?" I asked.

"Fine," she replied. "I've been working on finishing up my classes for this semester."

"Auntie told me all about you on the ride home -- done got all educated on me," I said.

"I'll be home tomorrow, so we can catch up. Don't let momma talk you deaf. Love you," she said before I handed the phone back to Aunt Shirl.

Well, after the call we headed out the door for our shopping excursion. Aunt Shirl was really concerned about my appearance -- "anorexic" was how she put it. I was kind of excited about going shopping and being able to pick out some clothes. Maybe I could find some personal items too, like after-shave and some manly deodorant. You know you've been out of touch with life for a while when you get a kick out of going to buy deodorant.

While we were shopping I was taking in all the sights and sounds of people doing something that they take for granted -- spending money on themselves, while enjoying the company of friends and family. It was really exhilarating for me to be a part of this experience, but at the same time I was feeling a little apprehensive. I've heard stories of ex-cons getting really paranoid in public places, almost to the point of having a panic attack. They think they're going to be mistaken for a criminal that was featured on the news or in a TV crime program.

While we were out, we made a trip to the grocery store. Aunt Shirl asked me what I liked to eat and I proceeded to tell her I wasn't a picky eater considering what I had grown used to the past five years -- runny oatmeal, lumpy grits, watery eggs and bran flakes. Oh, and once a week the chef, if you could call him that, would throw in some uncooked sausage and bacon. She had this awful look of disbelief on her face as she loaded the shopping cart with groceries for the coming week.

We spent about two hours on our shopping spree, trying on clothes and gathering the other items necessary for me to be considered an accepted member of society again. Actually, I was glad it was over and I couldn't wait to get home and take a bath and go to bed. "Lifestyles of the Rich and Famous" -- that's me.

By the time we pulled into the driveway it was starting to get dark. I went straight to my room, one that was like a suite in a five star hotel compared to what I had been used to in prison. I took a long hot bath...heaven on earth. Not a cold shower with a regulated time slot.

Aunt Shirl came in just as I was getting into bed and promised me that we would sit down and have a conversation about what I felt like I wanted to do with the rest of my life. That's a loaded statement for an 18-year-old who, for the past five years, has not had the liberty to make even the most basic decisions concerning the quality of his life. Of course I had dreams, but how to realize those dreams was a challenge I wasn't not quite sure how to face. I just shrugged.

"Everything will be okay," she said, and gave me a reassuring hug and a kiss on the cheek. "Tomorrow's a new day and I'm going to need some help in the shop. You game?" she asked.

"Sure," I said. "I don't mind at all. Just wake me up."

What a restful night I had. No flashlights shining over my head, no inmates making disturbing noises, and no harsh voices coming over the intercom screaming, "Count time."

As it turned out I didn't need a wakeup call. For the past five years I had been programmed, literally, to be an early riser. As I got ready, I thought about the long lines of inmates waiting their turn to use the bathroom. I realized these were things that most people take for granted, but for me it was just another miracle I had been blessed with in my new experience of life called freedom.

"Good morning Ryan," Aunt Shirl said as I made my way into the kitchen. "You're up bright and early. Did you sleep well?"

"Good morning Auntie. Yup, I slept just fine," I said as I headed to the coffee pot.

"I can make your favorite omelet, you know the one with the smiley face made out of catsup," she said with a smile.

I gave her a wide grin. Wow, she remembered my favorite breakfast from when I was just a small boy. "Thanks," I said. "Cereal will be just fine." I paused. "Aunt Shirl, can I ask you something?"

"What is it Ryan?" she responded.

"Well, what happened to those..." Before I could get another word out, in comes Cousin Terrance talking all loud. He cut me off in the middle of my sentence. I had gotten the nerve up to ask her what happened to the pictures of me and my family. Granted, I knew I was much older now and the pictures were no longer current, but it seemed to me at the time if they really wanted me to feel like a member of the family there would be a picture or two of me. And my parents. Maybe I was making more of this than I should. I was really hyper-sensitive to the vibes I was getting...you know, trying to read between the lines of what was being said or not said.

"Hey cuz, I see mom took you shopping to her favorite stores," Terrance said jokingly. "Mom, I can't believe you got that boy dressed up in stripes and khaki pants. Ain't no way my cousin is leavin' out this house lookin' like that."

"Shut up Terrance," Aunt Shirl interrupted. "Ain't a thing wrong with what he's got on. He looks just fine," she said as she looked at me and smiled.

"Cuz, don't worry, I got the hookup at some stores in the mall. We'll swerve by there later and pick you up some fresh gear," Terrance said with an air of confidence. "Mom, I'm hungry," he said as he sniffed around the bagel and cream cheese on her plate.

"Boy, get away from me...smellin' like you been up all night," she said as he reached across the table for the food that was on her plate. "Get upstairs and take a shower. We've got work to do at the shop. I need to you deliver some orders today."

"OK mom," he said as he grabbed the box of cereal from the table.

Terrance was a couple years older than I was, and quite the momma's boy. I guess it would be hard for him not to be, considering how she catered him. That boy had it made. A sports car that I'm sure he didn't pay for, pricey clothes...and that's just what I could see. Considering the world I just came from, Terrance lived like a king. I still wasn't quite sure if this was a mother's love, or if he was just a spoiled brat. Maybe it was a little bit of both. Hey, what did I know about a mother's love anymore? My mom had been dead for years. Still, with all the imperfections, it was a level of acceptance and caring that I had not seen in a long time -- one that I longed for.

I didn't get the opportunity to talk to Aunt Shirl about the pictures. Mornings in any home are hectic, and we were all rushing to get to the bakery and open up on time.

When we arrived at the shop and I hardly recognized it. Business was good, quite good. Aunt Shirl had expanded and upgraded. What once could have been described as a "hole in the wall" now resembled an upscale restaurant. The entry way was much more glamorous than I had remembered. Tables and chairs had been added so customers could enjoy a beverage while they indulged in the "goodies" from the oven. There were even tables outside, complete with colorful umbrellas. "Wow!" was all I could say. What a difference a few years could make.

"The shop looks great, Aunt Shirl. I love the new look," I said.

"Thank you Ryan," she said with a wide grin. "Nephew, I need you to put up the 'open' sign, and turn the lights on."

If anyone knew this business, Aunt Shirl did. She was definitely a talented baker with an imagination for unique creations, but she also had a business savvy, and knew how to turn her dreams into reality...one that brought a hefty profit.

The shop smelled like heaven...cocoa beans, coffee, chocolate, nuts; all rolled into one. It reminded me of the scent of the letter she had written to me while I was at Camp Penitude. Only much stronger, and better.

Through the day, I was really enjoying myself and was hard-pressed to call it work. I took orders, answered the phone, made coffee and even helped Cousin Terrance load the van for delivery orders. Even sweeping and mopping were a pleasure. It felt good to be a part of something meaningful and productive, but much more than that, it felt so wonderful to be doing something as a part of a real family.

The time just seemed to fly by, and before I knew it, it was time to close up for the day. Aunt Shirl and I had a moment to sit down and enjoy a honey nut brownie and a coffee.

"Ryan, what do you think of the shop? Do you think you would be interested in helping out, at least until you figure out what you want to do with the rest of your life?" Aunt Shirl asked.

What 18-year-old really knows the answer to that question? Today was the only day I could handle.

I tried to act like she hadn't caught me off guard and replied quite matter-of-factly, "Sure, I'd be glad to. After all, the fringe benefits are great," I said as I eyed the brownie. "I would like to get my drivers' license and eventually buy my own car so I won't have to depend on you so much."

"Well, I don't know if my nerves can handle teaching one more teenager how to drive. You see these gray hairs?" she asked as she pointed to her temple. "These are thanks to Terrance and Tonia and what they put me through when I was teaching them how to drive."

Well, I thought, I guess I'll have to learn from someone else. Just then Aunt Shirl winked at me, giving me the assurance that she would somehow see to it that she indeed would get me past the treacherous learning curve of drivers' ed.

And just like that, out of nowhere she asks me, "Did you have something on your mind, something you wanted to talk to me about?"

It kind of caught me off guard, but actually I did have something I was dying to ask her. As I swallowed the last bite of my brownie I managed to ask, "Yesterday as I was walking through the living room, I noticed the pictures of my family were no longer on the mantle, and come to think of it, my picture was no longer on your fridge; any explanation for that, Aunt Shirl?"

Auntie paused for a moment while she took off her glasses. She looked me straight in the eye and said, "Ryan, those pictures haven't gone anywhere. They are hanging up inside my office if you must know." Her tone of voice told me that I had struck a nerve with that question. She continued with her explanation: "After the painters finished up I decided on a little different décor for the house, thanks to input from my decorator daughter Tonia. Frankly Ryan, my life has been a little hectic the past few years. My business has gone from a small store front to a business that serves most of the people in my community. Since Matt died, it's all been on me -- managing employees, ordering supplies, baking, sales, advertising..." She paused for a moment to regain her composure. "Granted this is a huge blessing, but not one that doesn't come without a huge responsibility," she said. "Tonia suggested that I hang the pictures in my office at the shop to give it a more personal touch. I value her input when it comes to these types of suggestions."

I didn't seem too sure about her answer, but I didn't want to push. I took a bite of my brownie.

"Well," she said as she wiped her mouth with her napkin and pushed her chair back from the table, "Are we finished here, or do you have something else you would like to talk about? If not, I have some important calls to make."

"No ma'am," I replied.

Aunt Shirl got up from the table and went towards her office. I couldn't help but think that she was hiding something from me. What was the real reason she took the pictures down? Was that related to the fact that she hadn't written to me all the years I was incarcerated? I guess one offensive question at a time was all she could handle. Maybe I was reading a little too much into this, but deep down I still wanted to know.

CLOSE ENCOUNTERS OF THE GOD KIND

"Better to be slapped with the truth than to be kissed with a lie."
--Anonymous

Sunday morning greeted me with bright sunshine streaming through the blinds of my bedroom and the smell of freshly brewed coffee and hazelnut bagels coming from the kitchen downstairs. If that wasn't an incentive to get out of bed on a Sunday morning, I don't know what was.

Considering how I liked to sleep in on Sunday mornings, one could easily discern that church attendance was not one of my usual habits. I still wasn't quite sure where I stood on the "God" dilemma. I knew that He was real, but I wasn't quite sure what He was all about. I had a lot of questions. Where was He when I was being brutally abused all those years? What about all the tragedy in my family? And, what about me, why am I here, where do I belong and what about my future? What I had heard about the love and compassion of God didn't fit in very well into this equation called "the life and times of Ryan Blake."

After showering and dressing I made my way down to the kitchen. Shirl was already up. She had told me the night before that she had a lot to do to get ready for the Blake family reunion later that afternoon. It'd been years since I'd seen any of these people and I honestly was not looking forward to it. Maybe I could think of a way to get out of it. Just as I was coming through the dining room, I stopped short of entering the kitchen when I heard Aunt Shirl talking on the phone.

"Carrol Jean," I heard Aunt Shirl say rather firmly, "why are you talking so negatively about our Ryan? He's your nephew as much as mine, and a part of our family whether you like it or not. I reached out to him through a letter while he was still in that horrible place, because I believed he deserves a second chance. I know our brother John would want that for his son."

Carrol was yelling on the other end of the line and I could hear every word. "Shirl, stop it, you make me sick with that nonsense," Carrol said. "That boy killed our brother, and you're letting him stay with you? That just beats all I've ever heard!"

I sensed the disbelief and frustration in her voice. Aunt Shirl hadn't realized I had just come downstairs and her whole conversation could be easily heard by anyone close by.

The conversation continued between my dad's two sisters.

"Well," Aunt Shirl said, "what do you suggest I do, throw him out on the street and tell him I made a mistake by letting him come here? You know perfectly well, our momma raised us to treat people better than that, especially family."

I could feel the tension level beginning to mount. I should have known better than to think that I could slip under the radar and become a member of this family again without some type of reaction. What an eye-opener this was. Not everyone was as enthusiastic as Aunt Shirl was to help me get my life back together again. I can't say that I blamed them. But still I had no point of reference for how they felt. I loved my dad as much as possible, considering what I was going through at the time, but I wanted to put the past behind me. This was going to be more challenging than I realized. There would not only be confrontations from family members, but also all the hurdles I had to overcome just to become a productive member of society again -- whatever that was.

Aunt Shirl continued with her telephone rant. "Momma believed that there was some good in all people, regardless of what they may or may not have done. Carrol, can't you see that Ryan's been through enough, and I sure don't want to be the one to hold a mistake he made as a scared and troubled 13-year-old boy over his head."

"Mistake, mistake!" screamed Aunt Carrol. "Have you lost your dag blasted mind?"

"No I haven't," Shirl said matter-of-factly. "I read over all of the evidence, and John did some pretty cruel things to that boy. I believe Ryan shot him in self-defense. I honestly don't see how he had any other choice. There were markings all over his body. You know how hot-headed some of the men in our family can get. Well, at least they get it honest. You remember some of the rampages dad used to go on."

Aunt Shirl was referring to my grandfather, who I barely remember. This conversation kept getting more interesting by the minute. As a small boy I remember hearing bits and pieces of his abusive past. Well, looks like this family was no stranger to domestic violence. It was becoming more and more obvious to me why some of them would want to act like I never existed.

"During the trial," said Aunt Shirl, "the evidence from Ryan's journal told of how John had handcuffed him to the bed rail for five hours because he was failing math. Who in their right mind would do something like that to their own son? Hang on, I've got to stir these beans on the stove. I'm putting you on speaker."

Aunt Shirl definitely didn't know I was there, and she definitely wasn't giving Aunt Carrol a chance to speak.

"Well I--" began Aunt Carrol.

"Well nothing," said Aunt Shirl, stirring the beans in the pot. "The District Attorney let me read Ryan's journal. He wrote down everything he was afraid of and all of his feelings. That boy even feared for his life at times. I was literally shocked to hear what Ryan went through at the hands of his father's drunken rampages. John sounded like a deranged lunatic. Home is supposed to be place of safety for a child, not a place of fear and torture!"

"Can I talk?" said Aunt Carrol.

"Sure, fine," said Aunt Shirl.

"Well, I don't know about all that, Shirl. I wasn't there to witness anything that went on, nor did I read any of Ryan's journal. For all I know it was just a cover-up to make him look like a helpless victim. Look, you're my favorite little sister and I'm going to do everything in my power to protect you. We just don't need to lose another family member trying to rescue some kid who may decide to act crazy if he's misunderstood or something. So don't get upset with me if I voice my opinion."

"Before I go I have one more question for you," Aunt Carrol said.

"What is it Carrol Jean?" Aunt Shirl asked, sighing.

"Have you told Ryan about our little secret?"

"No!" she said emphatically. "That boy just got here two days ago and he needs some time to get adjusted. I'll tell him when the time is right."

I had no idea what she was talking about, but from her tone of voice I got the impression that my family had some more skeletons in closet. Well, at that point I couldn't say that it surprised me. What family doesn't have its granddads, uncles and fathers, and yes even sons, who bring shame to the family name? I guess I might as well get used to being no different than any of the other men in the Blake family. This phone conversation had really opened my eyes to what had been happening in my family.

Once Aunt Shirl had said her good-byes to her sister, I figured the coast was clear and made my way into the kitchen. Shirl was spreading something on a cracker and topping it with an olive. "Is anything wrong, Aunt Shirl?" I asked.

"Not really Ryan, I've just got a lot on my mind. I was just talking to Aunt Carrol Jean," she said, not looking up as she prepared appetizers for her afternoon guests. "You remember her don't you?"

"Yeah," I said. "Is she the one that has a different wig on her head every time you see her?"

What I really wanted to say is she the one that hates my guts for killing her little brother, but I held my tongue. I just grabbed a bagel and a glass of milk and made my way to the table. As I was woofing down my breakfast, Aunt Shirl informed me that since I was the newest member of the family, there was yet another tradition she expected me to be a part of. The expectation was that I would attend Sunday morning worship with them. Then she went on about our family heritage and foundational faith -- things I really didn't understand.

Well, I figured I could humor Aunt Shirl. What harm could a little church service do anyway? Especially if it kept Aunt Shirl happy. I was glad that I'd put on my new kakis and pullover collared shirt that I'd picked up at the outlet store a couple of days ago. I really didn't have much of a choice since my jeans were in the laundry. My new duds were the best clothes I had considering Terrance had yet to take me on the shopping spree he promised me. I guess my new "church uniform" would do for this one visit. I certainly wasn't planning on making this a habit.

Tonia, and to my amazement Cousin Terrance, arrived at the "Landfall United Methodist Church" at the same time as Aunt Shirl and me -- just in time for the service. I felt a little strange, kind of out of place to say the least, but everyone went out of their way to make me feel welcomed. Deep down I'd hoped the warm welcome wasn't a cover-up. I wondered how much of my past Aunt Shirl had let them know about me. Did they know that I was a murderer? Did they know that I was an ex-con? Did they know I was this very scared young man hoping that no one knew the truth about me and that all I wanted was to get through this "church thing" and go home and watch football?

The worship music was mostly traditional Gospel hymns, but to tell you the truth, I kind of enjoyed them. After the announcements and the offering Pastor Taylor ascended to the pulpit to deliver his message. He was a tall, thin white man with a Jersey accent. I guessed was probably in his mid-thirties.

That morning's sermon was entitled "Imitating our Fathers." I could tell Aunt Shirl was mesmerized by what he was saying by the way her eyes were fixed on him as she hung on his every word. Judging from her reaction, I believed she actually thought this sermon may have been an explanation for the physical abuse that was so prevalent in our family. Occasionally I would see her jot some notes down in the margins of her Bible. I had always thought it was considered sacrilegious to write in a Bible, but she was highlighting Scriptures and writing all over it. Oh well, what did I know about church, sermons and Bibles?

I noticed that when Aunt Shirl wasn't transfixed on the Pastor or her Bible that she would steal a glance my way -- I think to see what my reaction was to the sermon. I really didn't know what to make of it. I just stared at him, sometimes connecting my past with what he was saying and other times in utter disbelief that this kind of a thing was in the Bible. I also wondered whether this whole thing was a setup -- whether Aunt Shirl had conned

Pastor Taylor into preaching this sermon on the chance that I might be there that Sunday.

After the sermon Aunt Shirl introduced me to Pastor Taylor.

"Hello Ryan," he said as he shook my hand with a firm handshake. "Nice to meet you son, I've heard a lot about you."

He looked me right in the eye and had a genuine smile of warmth and acceptance on his face. I felt a little uncomfortable in his presence, seeing as I thought the whole sermon was directed towards me. If this was what church was all about I wasn't sure I wanted to come back.

"Thank you Pastor, I enjoyed your sermon this morning," I said.

I felt like that was the appropriate response, even though I didn't quite know how to process everything I had just heard.

"I heard you mention the term 'generational curse' and I'm not really sure I know what that means. To tell you the truth Pastor, you kind of lost me on that one. If you've got a few minutes I'd like for you to explain that to me if you don't mind."

"Sure Ryan," he said. "Give me a few minutes so I can shake these last few hands and I'd be glad to explain that to you."

He stepped to the side and politely greeted the congregants, shaking their hands, smiling graciously and hugging babies. He looked more like a politician than a Pastor.

"Thanks for your patience Ryan," he said when he was done. "Let me see how I can explain this to you in a way that you can understand. A lot of well-meaning Christians have misinterpreted the key verse I used in my sermon, that being Exodus 20:5-6. I know you're far from being a Bible scholar so let me paraphrase that verse for you. God is very gracious and longsuffering towards us while we continue headlong in our rebellious sinful ways. Each one of us is ultimately responsible for the choices we make in this life. If we sin, the Lord is always more than willing to forgive us of our iniquities and transgressions. That is, if we repent. Through faith in what Christ accomplished for us on Calvary, we are redeemed from the consequences of our sins, that being death and eternal alienation from God. But at the same time by no means will He excuse those who refuse this offer of forgiveness."

Pastor Taylor continued with his explanation, "People mistakenly believe that the Lord curses the children of parents who rebel against His commands. Granted, children will imitate the behavior of their parents, especially their fathers', because God designed us to do just that. He ultimately wants us to imitate Him, our Heavenly Father. But, if they read the Scripture carefully they will see that God visits the iniquity of these parents upon the children of the third and fourth generation of them that 'hate' the Lord and stubbornly persist in their rebellion...not those that love Him and in remorse cry out for mercy and forgiveness."

I just stood there staring at him like a deer caught in the headlights. It was a little overwhelming for me to process all that he had just said. I guess he took my pause as a cue to continue with his explanation.

"Ryan," he said rubbing his chin, "It's a documented, scientific fact that certain physical diseases can be inherited through the bloodline and passed on to the children of the next generation. Cancer and heart disease are just a couple of the big ones that come to mind. People tend to put all addictive behaviors like alcoholism and drug addiction into this same category. Although a child will have the propensity to follow in this example, if he never takes a drink or uses a drug, he eliminates the possibility of becoming addicted. Sin is a very serious issue with God, with very serious consequences. I know many people whose lives have been ruined by drugs and alcohol because they refused to take the dominion the Lord gave them over these substances. Now these substances, the herbs of the field and grapes of the vineyard, have the dominion over them."

"Wow," I said, "I never heard anyone explain it to me like that before."

I was a little hesitant to tell him what I'd been pumped full of in jail for the past five years. Just about everyone there believes they are the victim of something; bad parenting, bad influence, bad luck...you name it. I knew all too well what happened to me and my response to the insanity I was subjected to. But, what Pastor Taylor was telling me kind of shifted more of that responsibility to me. Before I had a chance to gather my thoughts and make a reply, he started talking again.

"Well young man," he said in a way that made me feel like he actually cared about me and wasn't just giving me the "God" speech, "let me give you just a little more insight into what I mean and then I'll hush. I don't want to overwhelm you with too much, this being your first day at church, but I feel compelled to go on."

I didn't know what happened to Aunt Shirl. I think she got carried away talking to some of the other women at the church. In a way I was glad. I just knew I was hanging on every word this man said. I knew it was Pastor Taylor's voice speaking to me, but somehow I felt like it was God speaking to me at the same time. I had never experienced that before. So, as you could imagine, I was mesmerized.

"My calling as a Pastor is first and foremost to shepherd God's people. Secondly, it's to bring them to a place of understanding about the Lord and His ways. I'm grateful when a young person like you comes to my church, someone who hasn't been 'churched' and unintentionally influenced by false teaching. God knows, we've got a lot of that to deal with. But I can tell by your response to my sermon, you're like an open book, hungry and eager to learn. When I was your age, I had a couple of setbacks and did some things that I'm not proud of. God, through the prayers of my parents, got a hold of me and I realized the error of my ways. After being restored to right standing with the Lord, God, through His grace, gave me a greater capacity to identify with some of the struggles young people like you face."

I was listening as intently as I could, hoping no one would interrupt us.

"Son," he said, "we are all responsible for the choices we make in life, and those choices come with consequences. I won't quote all the Scriptures to you, but in many places in the Bible the

Lord tells us that we are accountable to Him for our sins. What people do, in an effort to appease their guilty conscience, is tell themselves that they're not answerable to anyone but themselves. They're so wrong. When a man sins he sins against God and to God he must answer. The good news is that we have an Advocate, someone who is willing to stand up for us and declare us 'not guilty' in the grand court room of God."

Now this was something I could relate to. But how could someone so guilty, as guilty as I was, be declared "not guilty," and who was this great lawyer in the sky? I guess he could tell by the look on my face that I understood, yet I really didn't.

So the mini sermon continued.

"God," said Pastor Taylor, "in His love and compassion for mankind, sent His only Son to die on a cross in our place as the sacrifice for our sins. This satisfied the wrath of God against repentant sinners, once and for all, when His Son Jesus became a curse for us as He hung on that tree. He bore it all, and defeated it all on the cross – all the sin, the disease, and the addiction. Now, He is seated at the right hand of the Father interceding on our behalf. This of course, is based on the faith we have in what He accomplished for us at Calvary. It's all about Jesus, Ryan. Salvation, deliverance and justification. Ryan, I'm going to leave you with that explanation for now. There's so much more that I could go into, but I feel like I've given you all your soul can hold for one day. Please make it a point to come back to church. I plan on going into more detail about some of the things we talked about in my upcoming sermons."

He put his hand on my shoulder much the same way I would imagine a dad would when reassuring his son, looked me in the eye, and then turned and walked toward the door.

I just stood there for a moment, trying to take in everything he said. It was so meaningful I felt like I should have written it down. Just before Pastor Taylor walked out of the door, Aunt Shirl came out of nowhere and said, "Just hold it a second you two."

She looked a little flustered, like she was in a hurry to get the Pastor's attention.

"Pastor Taylor," Shirl said, "I know this is kind of short notice, but we're having our family reunion this afternoon at the house. I'd like to extend an invitation to you and your family. We'd love for you and Darla to come and catch up with what's been going on in the family this past year."

"Well Shirl, I'm afraid we're going to have to pass. This afternoon the Mrs. and me are driving up to Norfolk to visit her parents. I sure hate to miss it though."

"I understand completely," Shirl said with the grin.

Deep down I was glad he wasn't coming. I figured it would be a "hot mess" with me meeting the entire Blake clan all at once. I didn't expect them to greet me with open arms considering that I had killed one of their own.

As Pastor Taylor made his way once again to the door, Aunt Shirl turned her attention to me. "Did you and the Pastor have a good conversation?" she asked.

"Yup," I said. "We talked about his sermon."

"Great. You know how I feel about the importance of church. I hope you're planning on making this a habit young man," she said. I just looked at her and smiled as we headed out the door to the car

A Family Tradition

"Tradition does not mean to look after the ash, but to keep the flame alive."
--Jean Jaures

After we got home from church, Aunt Shirl and Cousin Tonia commenced to busying themselves with the final preparations for the monthly Blake family reunion. They were putting the finishing touches on specially prepared dishes, setting the table with the Sunday china, and making sure everything was "just right." In a matter of moments, people from all over town, and out of town, would begin to congregate for fun, fellowship and catching up with one another. I wasn't so sure how excited I was about all of them catching up with me.

This had become a tradition that dated back some 50 years, one that our Grandma Louise had started when she worked as a housekeeper for the Sterberg family. Once a year our family would set aside time from their normal routines and hectic schedules to meet for a special "reunion dinner." She had observed how the gatherings helped the family stay close and how it had allowed them the benefits staying connected with one another, regardless of the demands of everyday life. Needless to say, from that time on, this tradition became ritualized in the Blake family household.

I was upstairs trying to regroup my thoughts while everyone was waiting for the guests to arrive. I was more than apprehensive about meeting these people, considering how the phone conversation between Aunt Shirl and her sister went earlier that morning. Maybe that was an isolated incident and I didn't have anything to worry about. I hoped so. Well, all I could do was hope for the best.

Before I knew it the house was all abuzz with all kinds of people talking, laughing and enjoying one another. Even with my door shut it was all I could hear.

"Ryan," Aunt Shirl hollered. "Are you coming down here? Everyone's dying to meet you."

As I walked down the stairs, people started coming out of the woodwork to greet me. Some of the people I remembered from years ago, and some of them I had never seen before. They were shaking my hand, hugging me and slapping me on the back saying things like, "Good to see you son."

I heard another say, "Wow, look at how you've grown."

I even heard someone else say, "My God, he looks just like his father."

Maybe they were just curious, but the way they spoke to me gave me a sense of relief, like this family was might accept me after all. I knew that for the most part this was a God-fearing family and from what I can remember most of them went to church. So I figured that "judge not" thing might be really coming in handy for me.

Then the inevitable happened. I heard a voice in the crowd say, "That's the one."

That comment made me feel like I was in a police lineup. I knew what they were referring to. I had killed a member of their family. That put a damper on the reception, to say the least, but I pretended not to hear it and did my best to hold my head up high and roll with the punches.

I noticed on the couch that there were a bunch of presents wrapped up in assortments of colored paper. It looked like Christmas. I wondered what they were there for – or if anything could be for me. Just imagining unwrapping a present made me feel better. I hadn't done that in years. On the dining room table was a spread of food, the likes of which I'd never seen before. There were all kinds of meats, side dishes, and desserts. There was no way Aunt Shirl and Tonia could have fixed all this food. I guess everyone chipped in and brought something to add to the menu. I was feeling better and better.

Everyone was milling about and talking a hundred miles an hour. Just then Aunt Shirl grabbed one of those fancy glasses only used for special occasions from off the table and began tapping it with her spoon. It wasn't long before she had everyone's attention that was in earshot.

"My dearest kin," she said. "I want to thank you all for coming out to the Blake family reunion. Today we are gathering together to honor all of our family members, those who are here today, and those who have gone on to be with the Lord. From the first family that God created in the Garden of Eden He has had a desire to express His love to us through the family unit. So, all of us, individually and corporately, contribute to the purpose, destiny and character development of one another. Over the years our family has endured trials and tribulations, births and deaths, and all kinds of struggles and triumphs. Through our faith in God, we have overcome adversity's darkest hours and have remained strong in our commitment to the Lord and to one another. At this time I would like for us to bow our heads and pay homage to the late Katherine Louise Blake who passed the torch to me and thereby made this day possible for all of us. Someday, this tradition will be passed to you," she said looking in the direction of her daughter Tonia. Then she continued, "Embrace these moments with dignity and respect, and count them as a privilege and an opportunity to shape the heritage of your own children and grandchildren."

The room was quiet.

"Now family, if I may," Aunt Shirl said as she looked down to her Bible, "I'd like to read a couple of verses of Scripture written by the Apostle Paul. These words come from the love chapter, that being First Corinthians chapter 13 verses 3 through 7."

She picked up her Bible and began reading, "And though I bestow all my goods to feed the poor, and though I give my body to be burned, and have not love, it profits me nothing. Love suffers long, and is kind; love does not envy; love does not parade itself, is not puffed up; does not behave rudely, does not seek his own, is not provoked, thinks no evil; does not rejoice in iniquity, but rejoices in the truth; bears all things, believes all things, hopes all things, endures all things."

She hesitated for a moment as she looked around the room. I could tell some of the kids were getting a bit restless. Aunt Shirl continued with what would be her final comments before we ate.

"Each of us will not be judged by the clothes we wear, the cars we drive or the homes we live in. Even though our family as a whole has never been considered rich from a materialistic standpoint, we are rich in tradition, with a strong Christian legacy and family heritage. We will ultimately be judged on the quality of our relationship with God and how we appropriate that love, by the way we treat one another. Now I'm asking you with all the love I have in my heart for each and every one of you, to work hard on maintaining a bond of love between each other and keep the Blake family heritage alive and well for generations to come. And Lord, we thank you for the food we are about to receive. Bless it to our bodies, and our bodies to your service. Amen."

It took me a moment to absorb all of what she said. Before I realized it, there was a tear welling up in the corner of my eye. Her heartfelt words gave me a sense of security, a sense of belonging that I had never experienced before. I felt like I was as much a part of this family as anyone else, regardless of my past and the questionable opinions some family members might have of me. The present moment was all that mattered, at least as far as I was concerned.

The judgment and downright rejection I feared from others never really manifested, well at least not in the way I thought it would. While I mingled with relatives and enjoyed talking with them, some were a little distant, while others embraced me wholeheartedly. I could hang with that, seeing that was my first family reunion in more than five years. I just chalked it up to the fact that maybe some family members had a lot more to process than others. I guessed I still had a lot to learn about family dynamics.

I really enjoyed sitting down at the table, eating a formal dinner with civilized people. I used to dream of moments like this when I was incarcerated. Just the feeling of being accepted among people who knew me and cared about me was more welcoming to me than the all the wonderful food on the table.

After I stuffed myself with Chipotle glazed ham, mac-and-cheese, green peas, maple pistachio carrots, salad, rolls and chocolate honey-nut pecan pie (with a dash of vanilla ice cream, of course), I politely excused myself from the table and went downstairs to the rec room. This was where most of the younger people were congregating.

Cousin Terrance and my other cousins Rick and Karizma were huddled together on the couch playing video games on their phones. I took a seat next to them and was trying to get in on the action, well at least as an onlooker. Even though Aunt Shirl had gotten me my own phone, I was at a loss about how to play video games, so I just acted like I was engaged. When I went to prison five years ago, it was still the "flip phone" days, so I was really quite fascinated with this new technology.

Just then Tonia came down the stairs, giggling and carrying on. I glanced her way to see who she was talking to and I made eye contact with the most beautiful young lady I'd ever seen in my life. I just stared at her, kind of dumbfounded. She had gorgeous, smooth skin. Her complexion could best be described as "dark chocolate." She had the prettiest smile and she lit up the whole room like a beautiful rainbow does the sky.

I was totally mesmerized and just sat there with my mouth wide open. I realized I was drooling. Oh man. I hoped this wasn't some girl I was related to and didn't remember. I quickly grabbed my sleeve and wiped my mouth, pretending I was clearing my throat at the same time.

I knew it had been a while since I had seen any young women that I had been so attracted to. Come to think of it, it had been a while since I'd seen many women at all, at least none my age, and certainly none that looked like this. I was secretly hoping I wouldn't blow it and say something stupid. Tonia and "black beauty" were heading my way, so I realized I had better think of something suave and sophisticated to say real fast.

"Cousin Ryan," Tonia said, "This is my friend from school, Heaven."

"Your friend," I said, but what I was thinking was -- "Heaven!!! Well, that's exactly what she looks like to me." What a beautiful name for such a beautiful woman.

I was trying to pull myself together and not act like I'd just been thrown for a loop.

"Yes," said Tonia, a giggle in her voice. "My friend."

"Nice to meet you," I said as I stretched out my hand to her.

"Well," Heaven said, "The pleasure's all mine, Ryan. I've heard a lot about you from Tonia. How do you like Wilmington so far?" she asked.

"Well, considering I've only been here for two days, I barely have had enough time to get adjusted. My Cousin Terrance promised me that he would show me around," I said. I was choosing my words carefully, trying not to open a can of worms to a woman I just met, and quite a beautiful one at that.

Heaven hung around for the rest of the evening and as I got to know her a little better, the attraction to her grew even stronger. We played a couple of games of chess together. She beat me on the first game and I won the second one. I was pretty impressed with her skill, considering I had thought myself an expert in the game. Cousin Tonia interrupted before we could finish the second game. I guess she wanted some "girl time" with Heaven.

Before Heaven walked away she said, "You know, I work part time in the registration department of UNC Wilmington campus. If you ever decide that you're interested in attending school there and you'd like a tour of the campus, I'd be more than glad to show you around."

Here was my chance to spend some time with what seemed like a perfect woman. I should have immediately jumped at the opportunity and made arrangements to tour the campus, regardless of my present intentions concerning college. I hadn't really considered furthering my education at that point, although I had to admit she did make the possibility more inviting.

I kind of halfway stammered through an excuse of not really being sure about the whole college thing. I told her I would think about it once I got settled in.

"Ok," she said. "When you make up your mind let me know, and I'll be more than glad to help you out any way I can." We exchanged phone numbers and I agreed to contact her. Maybe I would consider college after all, I thought to myself.

I spent the rest of the evening enjoying time with friends and family. We exchanged some of the gifts that were on the couch, sharing laughs and hugs with one another. Cousin Tonia had informed me that part of our family tradition was to give gifts to one another at the reunion to make up for any missed birthdays. Each family member would draw names and get a gift for that person. I felt kind of bad about not having a gift for anyone and wondered again if there would be a gift for me. I was a little late getting in on the whole family reunion thing.

The strangest thing happened while everyone was passing the gifts back and forth to one another. Aunt Shirl casually handed me an envelope as she walked over to hand off a brightly-wrapped present to great-aunt. I noticed there was no name on the envelope and when I opened it, I couldn't believe my eyes. It was full of cash. I looked again and then I pulled out a wad of $100 dollar bills. I just kept counting until I realized that some anonymous person in my family had just given me $5,000. I couldn't believe it. I couldn't imagine who would do something like that for me. The only clue was a short handwritten note. It read:

Ryan,

I'm sorry I couldn't be there in person to meet you. Hope this money will come in handy to help you buy some personal things you may need to get started in your new life.

Love,
Family

I asked Aunt Shirl who could have possibly written this letter. The circle of family members grew quiet. Down the hall, I could hear a couple of little cousins squealing.

After what seemed like an eternity she responded. "Ryan, son, I don't have any idea who placed that envelope with the other gifts. I wish I knew. It was someone who wants to bless you and for whatever reason has chosen to remain anonymous."

That was the only explanation I got.

ONE MORE HURDLE

"Obstacles are the things a person sees when he takes his eyes off the goal."
-- E. Joseph Cossman

Monday morning came a lot sooner than I had anticipated. I already knew before I left prison I had to come to terms with post release supervision -- parole officers, that is. This is under North Carolina General Statue 15A-1368. The only reason I knew that is because it was drilled into me during the classes I attended prior to my release. Given that my residency was going to change from Virginia to North Carolina, my case manager had arranged for the transfer of supervision.

I had an appointment that morning at 8:30am at the parole board in the Law Enforcement Center in downtown Wilmington. With all the excitement of the past weekend, I had forgotten to set the alarm on my phone. Instead, I woke up to the sound of Aunt Shirl banging on my bedroom door. I realized I could get used to this sleeping in thing.

"Ryan, it's 7:20," she said. "Get your butt out of that bed before you're late for your parole meeting."

"Yes ma'am," I said, as I rolled over with a deep sigh of resentment. I begrudgingly got up and got ready. "Give me ten minutes." This wasn't something that I was looking forward to, but nonetheless a necessary evil. I got ready in record time. Kind of reminded me of my Camp Penitude days. We only had so many minutes to shower, shave and dress.

When I got downstairs Shirl was on the phone talking to Terrance and giving him some last minute instructions about opening the bakery. Deep down I was glad that she was going to be with me for this first meeting, although I didn't let on to her about that. After all I'm a man, or at least I hoped I had everyone thinking that I was. I quickly slipped by her and headed straight for the kitchen. I needed something on my stomach, something I could "grab and go." I grabbed a muffin Aunt Shirl had brought in from the bakery. As I ate it standing, I could hear Shirl in the other room giving instructions to Terrance about the old code for the alarm. Between my big bites I could make out something about it being reprogrammed.

I was just shoving the crumbs into my mouth when Shirl walked into the kitchen. I guess I looked like I'd been caught red handed or something. She glanced my way, smiled and said, "Boy, what am I going to do with you?" She grabbed her keys off the counter and we both rushed out the door together.

Morning traffic was hectic as usual. Shirl pulled some pretty nifty moves, dipping and dodging in and out of the traffic. She definitely didn't want me to be late for my appointment, especially since it was the first one. We arrived at 8:20 with just enough time to find a parking space. From the looks of it, this was a pretty busy place. We entered the building, found our way to the reception area, and realized we were fifth in line to be registered. We waited patiently as the parolees entered a door labeled "Do not Enter unless Authorized" as their respective names were called. The line moved fairly quickly and Shirl and I were at the receptionist's window in no time.

"Can I help you?" the receptionist asked in a pleasant voice.

Shirl spoke up before I had a chance. Part of me wished she would let me handle this. After all, this was my problem, not hers. I guess it was her mother instinct kicking in.

"My nephew, Ryan Blake, received instructions to report here," Shirl said as she motioned me to the desk.

"Yes, thank you ma'am," the receptionist said. "Just give me a moment while I look up his file."

The receptionist typed in a few things and scrolled down until she found my name.

"Oh yes," she said, "he's scheduled to meet with Mr. Weston. Please have a seat in the waiting area and he'll be with Mr. Blake in a moment."

At 8:45 am a short, bald man with a light complexion came through the "Authorized Only" door and said, "Mr. Blake...Ryan Blake."

Shirl and I both stood up and headed towards him. I bet we looked like a pair of twins conjoined at the hips. As we got closer, I could tell by the look on his face that Shirl was probably not as welcome as she thought she was.

"Mr. Blake," Mr. Weston said as he reached out to shake my hand, "may I ask, who's the lady accompanying you?"

Shirl quickly interjected, "Oh, I'm sorry Mr. Weston, I'm Ryan's aunt, Shirl Grason. Ryan is my nephew and he'll be staying with me."

"Ok, that's fine," Mr. Weston said, "Come on then."

We followed him to a cubicle in the far right hand corner.

"Both of you please have a seat while I pull up your file," he said, motioning to the two chairs in front of his desk.

I was scanning his office and desk to see if I could spy a picture or something to give me an inclination of his character. Nothing. All I saw was a pencil holder, a stapler and a cup of coffee that looked forgotten. You'd be surprised what you can tell about a person by how they decorate their office. You can usually tell if they're married, have children, if they're a Christian, and even what hobbies they have. Nothing. I studied his plain white shirt, blue tie and khaki pants. This guy either was the most boring person on the planet or he just didn't care to reveal anything personal about himself to us parolees.

I noticed Shirl was craning her neck trying to read Mr. Weston's computer screen. It's a wonder she didn't hurt herself the way she was stretching her neck all around like a giraffe. I was a little embarrassed, but said nothing.

"Ok Mr. Blake," Mr. Weston said, "it looks like your case file was transferred here from Virginia and you have the pleasure of having me as your parole officer for the next nine months. Let me first ask you some questions about your crime and then I'll be able to brief you on what I'm going to expect of you for the duration of your supervised parole. Fair enough?"

"Yes sir," I answered.

"I'm going to read off a transcript of your crime report and you tell me yes or no to the facts. The report states that on April 21, 2010, your father was Sherriff John Blake of Brunswick County Virginia when your mother, Theresa Blake, was killed in an auto accident, after which your father became depressed and started consuming excessive amounts of alcohol in order to cope. At some point, he shifted the blame for her death onto you because she was on the way to your school when the auto accident occurred. Evidently the principal had called her to come pick you up due to a disciplinary problem with at school. Correct so far?" he asked.

"Yes sir," I answered.

Mr. Weston continued reading the report:

"While on the way to the school your mother, Theresa Blake, was struck and instantly killed by a drunk driver. Shortly after her death the verbal and physical abuse towards you from your father, John Blake, began and continued escalating in frequency and intensity. On September 7, 2010 your father, John Blake, came home after he had consumed a considerable amount of alcohol. Still good, Ryan?" Mr. Weston asked.

"Yes sir," I answered nodding.

"Ok Ryan, I'm almost through with this section of our meeting. While you were with him in the home, again that was September 7, 2010, he became so violently abusive towards you that you feared for your life. So you grabbed the gun he kept in the nightstand in his bedroom and shot him in self-defense in the chest at point blank range. John Blake was found unresponsive at the scene by the paramedics and pronounced dead at Brunswick County Hospital at 12:02 am on September 8, 2010. Is everything that I've read thus far true?" Mr. Weston asked.

I looked over at Shirl and noticed that she was staring at the floor. I guess she was reliving these horrible moments too.

I responded, "Yes it is sir. Everything that you've read is accurate."

"According to your judgment and commitment paper you pled guilty to voluntary manslaughter and received a 60 to 84 month sentence. You completed 60 months at Camp Penitude for juveniles. Your prison record looks very good. You completed your GED, participated in anger management classes, Thinking for Change classes and Introduction to Computers. Also, Dr. Grimes, the resident psychiatric social worker, states here that you successfully completed her Skill Building Workshop and she also noted that in her opinion the chances of you returning to prison were slim to none. I do not see any record of disciplinary infractions or any negative reports from any correction's officials."

"Well Ryan, here's the good news in all of this," Mr. Weston continued. "From your prison record it does not appear as though you'll be a troublemaker and that's going to make my job a lot easier. However, I must warn you I've seen many ex-cons who get out of prison and inadvertently wind up with the wrong crowd. I don't think it's always intentional, but it happens nonetheless. They wind up messing around with drugs and alcohol and never report for their parole meetings, nor do they pay their fines. I don't take any pleasure in reporting violations, but I've got a job to do too and I'm sworn to enforce these policies. With that said Ryan, I will read you the terms of the conditions for your post-release supervision."

"1. Do not use, possess or control any illegal drugs or controlled substances unless it has been prescribed for the supervisee by a licensed physician.

2. Comply with a court order to pay court costs and costs for appointed counsel or public defender in the case for which the supervisee was convicted.

3. Not to possess a firearm, destructive devise or other dangerous weapons unless granted written permission by the Commission or post release supervision officer.

4. Report to a post release supervision officer at reasonable times and in a reasonable manner, as directed by the Commission or post release supervision officer.

5. Permit a post release supervision officer to visit at reasonable times the supervisee's home or elsewhere.

6. Remain within the geographic limits fixed by the Commission unless granted written permission to leave.

7. Promptly notify the post release supervision officer of any change of address or employment.

8. Remain in one or more specified places for a specified period each day and wear a devise that permits the defendants compliance with the condition to be monitored electronically.

9. Submit at reasonable times to searches of the supervisee's person by a post release supervision officer. Whenever the search consists of testing for the presence of illegal drugs the supervisee may also be required to reimburse the Department of Corrections for the actual cost of drug testing.

10. Pay supervision fee of $30.00 per month."

After Mr. Weston read off these rules he asked me if I understood the terms of the agreement or if I had any questions. He also motioned for me to sign at the bottom of the page.

I glanced over at Shirl to see whether or not this was something I should sign.

She quickly interrupted and said, "I have a few questions Mr. Weston. My nephew may be attending college. We need to know if that will interfere with his probation or not?"

"Not as long as long as he lets me know where he will be staying and if he'll be playing any kind of sports. Call and tell me if and when you will be leaving town so I can get approval from my supervisor," Mr. Weston said.

"Okay," Shirl said. "And what about an ankle monitor? Will he have to wear one?"

"Usually I make my supervisee's wear one, that is if they have a violent charge. However, I'm a firm believer in giving everyone a second chance until they prove to me that they can't be trusted. After having read over Ryan's case file I don't think that he will pose a problem. Do you?" he asked Shirl.

Shirl shook her head and said, "Absolutely not sir!" Then she mumbled to herself, "If he should get out of line I'll bring him to you."

I signed and dated the paper. I shook Mr. Weston's hand and he handed me his business card. Shirl fumbled through her purse and found her business card which she promptly handed to Mr. Weston.

I had just completed my introduction to post release supervision. Oh well, I thought. All of the rules and stipulations are pretty much common sense to any law abiding citizen, which I did consider myself to be. It was only for nine months and I didn't see any problems with compliance.

Shirl and I walked out of Mr. Weston's office and walked through the reception area to the exit.

COLLEGE BOUND

"I never let my schooling interfere with my education."
-- Mark Twain

Life continued to evolve fairly normally, well that is if there is a definition for "normal" in my world. Over the course of six months I was able to get my drivers' license and buy a fairly decent used car with the money the mysterious anonymous donor had given me at the family reunion. I wasn't quite sure what to make of this undercover giver, but I sure wanted to meet him or her one day and thank them personally. Sometimes I wondered if "he" wasn't Aunt Shirl. But she promised me she wasn't, and she just didn't seem capable of telling me a lie.

I had also managed to get through most of the nine months of my probation without an incident. Sadly, some parolees make the wrong choices and become another statistic of the system. They violate their parole or break a law and the prison system becomes nothing more than a revolving door to them. I was determined that was not going to happen to me. The time I served at Camp Penitude was a literal hell on earth and worked as a very good deterrent for me.

At my most recent visit with my probation officer, Mr. Weston suggested that I find ways to volunteer my time in serving my community. He said it would be a good gesture, my way of giving back to the people who were willing to give me a second chance. At first I was at odds with the suggestion. I felt like I had paid my debt to society and that I didn't owe anyone anything. Boy, did I have a lot to learn.

My first class in community service education came a few days later when Pastor Taylor hit me up. He called and asked if I'd be willing to help the youth refurbish the Sunday school building's leaky roof next Saturday. My gut response was to decline, but on second thought I realized what an embarrassment this would be to Aunt Shirl if I refused a man of God. It would probably disappoint the Pastor too, so I begrudgingly agreed.

Saturday morning rolled around and I was about to embark on my first real experience with serious manual labor. I was a little apprehensive because I wasn't sure how much the other teens knew about my past and whether they would accept me or not. People were bound to talk about me, I just wasn't sure what they were saying. I'd just have to suck it up and hope for the best.

When I arrived at the church I was about 30 minutes late because I forgot to set the alarm on my phone...again. Man, I needed to work on that. Nothing like being late to make yourself conspicuous. Anyway, all the teens, Pastor Taylor included, were busy working on the roof. They looked like a bunch of ants crawling around up there. Pastor Taylor happened to look my way and motioned for me to come closer. He quickly crawled down the ladder and walked toward me with his right arm extended. "Glad you're here Ryan. Good to see you," he said with a firm handshake.

"Please forgive me for being late Pastor. I overslept," I said.

"You're good son, don't worry about it," he said.

I was wondering who all the guys were on the roof and how I would fit in. Pastor Taylor must have sensed my apprehension and put his arm around my shoulder.

"Guys, guys!" he shouted looking up toward the roof. "Ya'll hold up a minute. I want to introduce you to Ryan Blake. He's gonna be working with us today."

"Hey Ryan," they all said in unison. "Glad you could make it!"

"Alright you guys, lay off. He's a newbie," Pastor Taylor said in my defense.

Nothing like making a good first impression was all I could think.

"You know anything about roofing?" he asked.

"Not really. I hammered a few nails when I was about nine years old," I said with a smile.

"Well, now's a good time to learn," he said as he handed me a tool belt with a crowbar looking thing and a hammer hanging from it.

I headed up the ladder behind him. Once on top of the roof, Pastor Taylor did some quick introductions.

"Ryan," he said, "This is Jake and his sidekick Steve."

"Hey guys," I said.

"They're a part of a mentoring program I sponsor for youth in the community. Good guys and hard workers." Pastor Taylor said. "And to my left are Vince and Eddie. They attend my church and are part of our youth program."

"What's up?" I asked.

They didn't look up and just kept right on working.

"Do you two want to say hello to Ryan?" Pastor Taylor asked.

I was a little embarrassed at the way Pastor Taylor was handling this. I felt like he was overreacting a little. I just thought they were too busy to look up, but maybe there was more to it.

"Look you two," Pastor Taylor said. They stopped what they were doing and gave him their undivided attention. "Ryan's no different than any one of you guys. He's on a journey of finding himself just like you are. So lay your judgments aside and show him how to strip these shingles off, ok?"

"Yes sir," they said.

"Come here Ryan," Vince said, "and I'll show you the ropes."

What an introduction was all I could think. Things kind of loosened up as the day wore on and I actually got to the place where I felt comfortable around Vince and Eddie and the other guys. We spent the rest of the day working hard and by late afternoon we had finished the roof. I actually enjoyed the hard work and being with these guys. Turns out the mentoring program the preacher sponsored was for "at-risk" youth, and they had their own horror stories about the things that had happened in their lives. Listening to them made me realize how fortunate I was to even get a second chance. Even though I still had a lot to learn when it came to life, work and relationships, I considered this experience a great lesson. Sometimes just being with other people and accomplishing something useful, regardless of what it is, can add volumes to your self-esteem.

Still, when I came off that roof, I knew I didn't want to do manual labor the rest of my life.

So later that summer I took Aunt Shirl's and Tonia's advice and took steps to enroll at UNC Wilmington for the fall semester. Along with all the regular paperwork of submitting applications, transcripts and placement tests, as an ex-con I was advised by Mr. Weston to submit a personal essay to the school registrar explaining my criminal record and my career goals. Tonia was gracious enough to help me with all of that. We submitted all the paperwork and hoped for the best. I had no idea my past would hang over me like a shadow. If attending college was this much of a challenge, I wondered what it would be like when it came time to apply for a job? I went through it all without asking Heaven for help. I was too nervous.

The day the acceptance letter came in the mail was a real blessing in more ways than one. Sure, I was relieved that my application and personal essay had been accepted, but even more than that I wanted to live up to my mom's expectations of me. With a trust fund for my education I was determined to graduate with a degree -- even though I still wasn't quite sure what I wanted to major in. I'd be the first one in the family with the last name Blake with a college degree.

September rolled around before I knew it. I had opted to live on campus, partly because the trust fund allowed me to, and partly because I wanted to experience everything college life had to offer. I was so full of anticipation -- the excitement of learning new things, meeting new people and being on my own for the first time in my life.

Since I hadn't declared a major yet I just registered for some general core classes, hoping that sometime in the near future I would find my niche in the college and professional world. I had no idea how many decisions had to be made when you actually had a choice concerning your destiny.

Once I had made it into school, I finally took Heaven up on her offer. She kept her promise and acted as my tour guide, showing me all the buildings that were on the campus. The place was huge. They had a building for everything -- a science building, an economics building, an engineering building. There were also all kinds of dorms and student activity buildings.

It was so cool to be walking around campus with this beautiful woman. It really made me feel like I was someone special. I couldn't believe that someone who looked like her didn't have a boyfriend, but she didn't. After the initial "tour date" I made it a point to contact her. We occasionally had lunch together and a couple of times I made references to how attracted I was to her, hoping that she would get the hint. She never responded in a positive way to any of my comments, so we just remained friends. I was a little disappointed, but not crushed.

Cousin Tonia stayed busy with a lot of extracurricular activities, school projects and the girls' volleyball team. She encouraged me to get involved in some of the many programs offered on campus, but wanted to stick with what I was familiar with. Basketball. So I tried out for the team as a walk on. There were a couple of other guys that tried out with me. The coach was really impressed with my defensive moves, but came down a little hard on me about my offensive strategy. I tended to "hog" the ball and wasn't as willing to pass it to the other players as I should have been. I guess you could chalk that up to immaturity. Unlike my junior ball days and the ball I'd played in prison, college ball was a whole new ballgame, literally. I was playing against some guys who had a very good possibility of going pro. I felt like I was up for the task though and was committed to work hard during the practices.

I found myself hanging out with the guys I played ball with. One in particular was my roommate, Quan Jeffery, a slick-talking city boy from the Bronx. He moved in right after I'd started practicing with the team, and right after my original roommate had left school for being homesick, something I couldn't understand.

Quan was quite the ladies' man, smooth talking them with his accent and empty promises. Quan was scholarship player. He was a decent ball handler and quick on his feet, with some pretty impressive moves. I'd observed his technique while we played scrimmages together. He stood about six feet tall and was able to cross up his opponent, switch directions on a dime, and do a mean fade away shot that swooshed right through the net. He had a sassy demeanor about him and stared down his opponent, almost daring them to stop his advances toward the basket. Quan was unstoppable both on the court and off.

One day after practice we were in our room tossing a foam ball into a hoop on our door. "Hey Ryan," Quan asked, "you want to go with me to a party tonight? Plenty of girls, booze, and drugs. Interested?"

"I don't know Quan," I said. "I'm really not into the party scene and besides, I was planning on going home this weekend. I had promised my Aunt I would help her out in the bakery this weekend."

His next statement was a little more persuasive.

"Come on man, your parents aren't even a part of the picture anymore. They can't nag you about things like this; you've got it made. Can't you make your own decisions? This is your chance to have some real fun and experience life at its best. Man, hasn't anyone told you yet that college is one giant social club? We've got it made in the shade man with all these young co-eds walking around. Just picture it, you and me partying with some of the most beautiful, vulnerable women this state has to offer. They breed these chicks like they do down on the chicken farm. There's plenty for all of us. You in or out, man?"

"Well," I said, "I guess I could show up and hang around for a little while, what harm could it do?"

I wasn't quite sure about what I was getting myself into, but I wanted to imitate some of Quan's charisma and charm with the ladies. Everyone looked up to him like he was some kind of a god or something.

That night I attended a number of parties. I caved in to the pressure of wanting to be accepted more that wanting to listen to my conscience. They proved to be everything Quan had promised -- sex and drugs and rock and roll. Everyone there was drinking some kind of beer, wine or liquor. There were scantily dressed women, with too much makeup, showing off their latest hair creations and hoping for the approval of one of us guys. Most of these young women were well on their way to getting drunk or under the influence of various drugs. They were flirting and flaunting themselves all over the men. These "hipsters" were dancing dirty, bumping and grinding to the loud music. Drugs were being passed around like candy. I think just about everyone there, men and women alike, were on something.

I was standing in the corner, checking out the scenery when this guy approached me and asked me if I wanted to buy some Molly. I refused because I didn't do drugs and quite honestly it scared me. I had no idea what this drug was and I certainly didn't want to risk being poisoned, becoming addicted, or even overdosing. Much less failing a drug test for my parole officer.

Just as I was beginning to get my composure, Quan came over and introduced me to a couple of young ladies, Kimberly and Courtney. They were two young co-eds who were evidently out looking to have some fun that night. I tried to give them the benefit of the doubt, but I had pretty much already judged all of these women as drunks who were easy prey in this "shark tank" we called a party.

Kimberly recognized me from our business ethics class. We had a brief conversation about our professor, Dr. Foley, and his unconventional teaching methods. He had recently retired from business and was pursuing a teaching career, I guess because he had too much time on his hands. His motto was "learn, commit and do." This was the method that contributed to his success in the business world and he assumed it would work in the classroom. All I knew was we all got a kick out of his peculiar ways and he was the butt of a lot of jokes from his students. Before I could say anything else to Kimberly, Quan rudely interrupted.

"Hey, you two want a beer?" he asked. He had a cold one in each of his hands. Kimberly accepted, but I declined. Years ago I had made a vow that I would never touch the poison that destroyed my father's life, and ultimately mine.

"Come on Ryan, one beer won't hurt," Quan said as he looked at me in disbelief.

"Nah," I said. "I don't want one. I can't stand the smell of the stuff." This time I looked him right in the eye and let him know that I meant what I said.

Kimberly saw how emphatic I was about not drinking, and I noticed out her quietly setting her beer down on the counter. I guess persuasion can go either way, even in this unpredictable environment where choices are so influenced by the pressure of peers. Touché; I thought, I killed two birds with one stone. I had now had earned Kimberly's respect and simultaneously gotten rid of a bad influence. Quan retreated to the dance floor, Courtney and beer in tow.

Kimberly and I made our out to the patio so we could continue our conversation without any further distractions.

"So Ryan," she said. "Tell me a little bit more about yourself. What brings you to UNCW?"

"Well Kimberly," I said. "Can I call you Kim for starters?"

"Yeah, sure," she said.

"Okay, you asked," I said. "My story is a little more complicated than most, but I'll give you the condensed version."

I noticed a smile come to her face as she leaned forward in anticipation of my reply.

"Of course, like everyone else I'm here to get an education," I said. "How I got to this place in my life is probably a lot different than how you did. You see, when I was a kid both of my parents died in a tragic accident. Since then I've been fortunate enough to have a lot of support from other family members, namely my Aunt Shirl. She's my dad's sister. She took me in and I guess you could say she's kind of adopted me as one of her own. I've received a lot of encouragement from her and others as well, to set goals for myself and to make every effort to achieve those goals."

Kim just stared at me with a look of bewilderment. "I'm so sorry to hear that," she said. I could tell she really meant it and that she had never encountered anyone who had experienced this.

Then she asked the ten thousand dollar question. "What happened to them?"

Looking away I said, "You sure do ask a lot of questions. We just met, and haven't even been talking with each other for over five minutes yet."

This was my way of trying to avoid the question. I'd never been asked this before, and quite honestly I'd never considered what would be the appropriate response. I didn't want to tell a boldfaced lie, and I didn't want to be completely honest either. So I did what I thought was best. I compromised and told half-truth.

"Kim," I said. "I don't mean to sound sarcastic, it's just that the death of my parents is a really sensitive subject. I'm not sure I'm ready to discuss this with someone I barely know. They both died when I was really young, and I haven't gotten to the point where I'm comfortable talking about what happened. I hope I haven't offended you. I really appreciate your concern though."

"I understand," she said. "I really didn't mean to pry."

Well I dodged the bullet that time. I hadn't considered that people would be curious about my parents' deaths. Eventually the truth would have to come out. I was just glad it wasn't right now.

After our brief conversation, Kim and I found our way back to the party to see what was going on with Quan and Courtney. We looked all over for them, but they were nowhere to be found. Kim seemed concerned because she and Courtney had agreed to never leave a party without each other, and definitely never to leave with a stranger without letting each other know where they were going.

Since Kim had ridden to the party with Courtney, I offered to give her a ride back to her dorm. We were both hoping that Courtney would be there. Kim agreed, if not somewhat reluctantly. I noticed Kim trying to call Courtney, but to no avail. She left her a voicemail letting her know we were leaving the party and on our way back to the dorm.

The short ride to the dorm seemed much longer than the ten minutes that it took. I was sure that was due to the fact that neither one of us spoke a word to each other. Too many "what ifs" were running through both our minds. There had been a recent sexual assault of young co-ed on campus and the assailant had yet to be identified. We tried not to think the worst, but considering what we were dealing with, it was hard not to let our minds drift towards those thoughts.

When we pulled into the dorm parking lot and didn't see Courtney's car, the worried look on Kim's face intensified. "Where could they be?" Kim asked with a look of fear in her eyes.

"Well, I can't call Quan. He busted his phone at practice today." I tried to calm her racing thoughts by offering some logical explanations. "Maybe they got bored at the party and decided to leave and catch a bite to eat," I said unconvincingly. "Or maybe they hooked up with some other people and decided to go to another party or a club. It's Friday night and they're probably out looking for a good time." This time I was a little more emphatic with my possible explanations. "She'll give you a call when she gets your message," I assured her.

She was still quiet.

"Hey listen," I said, "if you don't hear from her, give me a call and we'll both go out and comb the neighborhood and some of the local bars and try to find her. Don't worry, I'm sure she's just fine," I said with an air of confidence.

As I texted my number to her cell phone I wondered if her fears were something I needed to consider or not. After all, the "person of interest" here was the man I shared a dorm room with and was someone I considered a friend. Not that I knew him that well. Kim was insinuating that Quan could possibly be a threat to Courtney's well-being. In my mind he was just a young guy full of energy looking to have a good time.

I left Kim at her place and drove home to my dorm hoping to find Quan and Courtney there. Well, my hopes didn't pan out quite the way I thought they would. The dorm was just the way we left it. It was obvious that no one had even been there since Quan and I had left.

Once on my bunk, I realized I was more tired than I thought. The college life had caught up with me. I had had all the classes, ball practice and partying I could take for the week. And besides, worrying about the fate of my friend and his companion had also taken its toll on me. I laid across the bed to get some sleep, still hoping that Quan would come through the door and all my fears and apprehensions could also be laid to rest.

The next morning I was awakened by my cell phone ringing. I glanced at the screen and realized it was Aunt Shirl's number. Oh no! I overslept. Once again. I was supposed to be at the bakery at 9:00! Man, I felt terrible. I didn't answer the phone because I wasn't in the mood for what I knew I would hear on the other end. I just knew that she was mad, but worse than that I had let her down. Well, no time for regrets now. I jumped out of bed, splashed some water on my face, got dressed and ran out the door.

It took me about 30 minutes to get to the shop. I rushed through the front door and immediately I saw Aunt Shirl standing behind the counter serving customers. I could tell by the look on her face that she was disappointed in me. I was grateful for the momentary "stay in execution" the customers provided. I guess she would let me have it once they left. I could see Tonia in the kitchen helping to train the new baker and Terrance was nowhere to be seen. He was probably running the deliveries I was supposed to be on.

The customers left and my moment of truth had arrived. I manned up, walked over to Aunt Shirl and apologized for being late. I explained to her that I had overslept, hoping that would suffice as a legitimate excuse. I really wasn't quite sure what kind of a reaction I would get, but I was hoping for a gracious one.

"Next time I call you Ryan, at least have the common decency to answer the phone," she said as she smiled and handed me an apron. My cousins had warned me of that smile. It's her way of letting you know she's angry or frustrated without expressing the feeling of her emotion. Kind of keeps you in the dark about what's really going on in her mind.

With that she headed to the back of the store, not giving me an opportunity for any explanation. She was right though. I could have at least answered the phone. What a coward I was, I thought. I felt disappointed in myself that I had let her down.

As the day wore on, you could literally cut the tension in the air with a knife. So I was quite relieved when a breath of fresh air walked through the front door -- Tonia's best friend and my hopeful friend-to-be, Heaven. She greeted me with a hello and a beautiful smile. Every time I saw this woman my heart skipped a beat. I was so smitten with her. The attraction was purely physical and she aroused feelings within me that I had never experienced when it came to women. Sure Kim had been cute and a lot of fun, but there was something unique about Heaven that attracted me to her. She was so poised and intelligent and had a such a passion for life that it was almost contagious. Deep down I was hoping I could somehow impress her. Maybe I could dazzle her with my charisma, my good looks, or my sense of humor.

Tonia interrupted my daydreaming when she greeted Heaven with a warm hello. She proceeded to inform her that another female student at UNCW had been sexually assaulted off campus last night. Immediately my thoughts went towards the unthinkable. Could it be Quan and Courtney? No way. Just a coincidence, I told myself, and I quickly dismissed that thought. I had spent five years of my life incarcerated with rapists and in my eyes Quan definitely didn't fit the profile.

Tonia continued with her conversation. "So, we're having a meeting this evening on campus. It will be in the East Yard at 5:30 in order to see if we can rally enough support for better security measures. We're going to request that all the women make sure that when they are walking on the campus grounds after dark that they pair up with a friend. As I was listening I felt compelled to offer my help in any way I could.

"Tonia, can I do anything to help?" I asked.

Heaven glanced my way and smiled with an amazed look on her face. I didn't know if my offer surprised her, or if she was flirting with me. I chose to believe the latter. Just then Tonia cut me a look as if she wanted to say, "Boy, please," but instead she said, "Sure you can help Ryan. See if you can get some of those vipers you hang around with to come to the meeting tonight. The more support we have, the better. We've got to make a statement that these crimes will not be tolerated."

"Vipers?" I said, surprised. "I'm all in to help," I said enthusiastically.

Just then Aunt Shirl interrupted and asked if she could speak with me in her office. She probably thought I was goofing off and laying down on the job. I politely excused myself and followed her rather sheepishly into her office.

"Close the door," she said without expression.

"What is it Auntie?" I asked.

Aunt Shirl commenced to let me have it.

"I think I deserve an explanation for why you were late for work this morning. I was counting on you to help Terrance with the deliveries. You made a commitment to me and I expect you to honor it. A successful business is only as good as the people who are a part of it. As far as I'm concerned there's no room for unexplained absences or tardiness. I don't tolerate it with my own children, and I certainly won't tolerate it with you. If you can't work your assigned shift, or if you're going to be late, the decent thing to do is to call and let me know. Now that I've said my peace, what do you have to say for yourself young man?"

"Well," I said, "for starters I'm really sorry for being late and for not answering your call this morning. I went out with a friend and he took me to several parties on campus."

At this point I wondered if she thought I was drinking or got high on something and passed out.

I continued with my plea. "I didn't get drunk or do anything stupid. It was just late when I got home and I forgot to set my phone to wake me up, and I overslept. There's no excuse for my behavior. Please forgive me. It will never happen again."

Aunt Shirl just stared at me without saying a word. I wasn't sure if she was going to burn a whole through me with her eyes, or yell at me or what. I couldn't imagine me being late this one time would throw her over the edge like that. I wondered if something else was bothering her.

It was an awkward moment. I just stood there, looking around and wondering whether I should man up and take what was coming to me, or make a beeline for the door. Just then I noticed the strangest thing sitting on her desk -- a manila envelope, and written on it in big black letters was my name and address. There was also a wad of hundred dollar bills right next to it. I couldn't help but think of the money that was given to me by an anonymous giver earlier that year at the family reunion. Aunt Shirl, seeing the expression on my face and realizing what I had seen, hastily grabbed the money and the envelope and shoved them in the top drawer of her desk.

"Boy," she said, "just pretend you didn't see that."

"What do you mean?" I asked.

Shirl was visibly shaken and doing all she could to gather her composure.

Then she managed to blurt out, "I mean...that's the deposit from today's sales. I should have never left it out on the desk like that. Now, don't you have some work to do?"

"Okay...whatever," I said as I turned and walked out of her office.

COULD THIS BE?

"Lord, please don't let me fall to someone who is not willing to catch me."

-- Anonymous

"Great job fellas," Coach Connors said with a broad smile on his face. "Another win and we're on our way to the playoffs."

Then he glanced my way with an apprehensive yet approving look and said, "Great defensive moves, Ryan, in stopping number 22 from driving to the basket and scoring." With that, Coach glanced over at Quan and said, "My only beef is that you dribbled the ball way too much in the last quarter instead of trusting in your teammates. We're a team, don't ever forget that."

I had to say that Quan looked little surprised at coach's demeanor, considering he was the lead scorer on the team. But I guess he was right. Sometimes Quan did get carried away during games when he got the ball, thinking he was a one-man team. The coach kind of lightened up a bit and said to us, "Next week we're up against the Eagles. We've got practice on Monday, and ya'll need to be ready to run some drills." Then he gave us that fatherly look and said, "Have a great weekend, and remember, stay out of trouble." Then we all shouted in unison as loud as we could, "United we stand, divided we fall, Go Seahawks!"

As we were getting our gear together, Quan approached me and asked, "Hey Ryan, some of the guys are going to a party tonight over in Echo Farms, you in or out?"

"For sure, count me in," I said without giving it a second thought. "I don't have to work in the morning, so I'm free to hang out late. Sometimes my Aunt Shirl can be a nag, riding my back about every little thing. It makes me feel like there's a tape recorder in my head replaying all of her warnings about things I should and shouldn't do."

Quan threw his head back and laughed out loud. "Boy, you're crazy," he said. "I'm so glad my parents live in New York, so I don't have to listen to all that noise. Speaking of noise, your armpits are screaming "bathe me...please, please."

"Man," I replied as I threw a towel in his direction, "You're the one who's crazy."

"Ok then," Quan said. "I'll catch up with you later at the dorm. I've got something I need to take care of first."

He grabbed his gym bag and headed out the door. As I was leaving the gym, Frankie Costner, a teammate of mine, stopped me and asked, "Hey Ryan, you got a minute? I need to talk to you about something."

"Sure, what's up?" I asked.

"I overheard you talking to Quan about you and him hanging out tonight," Frankie said.

"Yah, what's wrong with that?"

Frankie hesitated for a second before he said, "I don't want you to think I'm a hater or anything, but you need to be careful hanging around with Quan -- he's bad news man."

I was wondering what he could possibly know about Quan that I didn't already know. After all, we shared a dorm together, took classes together and even played ball on the same team.

Frankie continued to fill me in on the gory details: "Talk around campus is that he's involved with some heavy hitters that have him selling drugs on campus. And if that's not bad enough there was a girl from our school who was intentionally drugged and sexually assaulted on campus last month. Get this -- it was a guy from our school and he claims he bought the pills from Quan. This 'informant,' who happens to be in one of my classes, was roughed up pretty bad by three guys the other night when he was leaving a party. He told me they warned him not to be spreading anymore 'rumors' about Quan's business ventures, or he'd suffer severe consequences."

I just stood there and stared at him in disbelief.

"So let me get this straight, because I'm having a little bit of a hard time processing what you've just told me. Quan Jeffery's a drug dealer? You must have the wrong guy. We live together man. Don't you think I would have noticed? And you're telling me I need to be careful! Look Frankie," I continued, "just answer me this one question, will ya? Why in the world are you telling me this? Why don't you go to Coach Connors?"

"Like I said, the last person that talked about this was threatened by some goon squad. I'm not willing to get my face bashed in. The only reason I'm telling you is because you're fairly new on the team and I don't want to see you get caught up in someone else's mess."

"OK, OK Frankie, I get it," I said. "Thanks for the head's up."

"For sure my man," he said as he gave me some dap on my fist.

I threw my gym bag in the trunk and got in the car. I just sat there for a few minutes pondering what I had just heard. Wow! What a bombshell he just dropped on me. I didn't know what to think. Quan, my roomie, teammate and classmate, under investigation for dealing drugs? They had to have him pegged wrong. I knew he was a little crazy, but a drug dealer? "No way", I thought to myself. How could I have missed this just coming out of prison? The last thing I needed was for someone to say "I told you so" after what I'd been through in the past five years of my life. Not to mention the fact that I still had three months to go before I was officially off the grid from doing prison time.

Hanging out with Quan was definitely out of the question. I considered finding a new roommate, but wasn't sure how to go about that without coming right out with the reason. It was just too much to think about at the moment.

This was not the way I wanted to start my evening. It was supposed to be a night of celebration. We had just beaten one of the best teams in the conference and the whole team was in party mode. I was contemplating my possibilities and looking for a way to ditch my plans with Quan. I certainly didn't want to sit in front of a TV all night, so after weighing my options I gave Kim a call. No luck -- voicemail. I decided not to leave a message.

I took a chance and gave Heaven a call. When she answered I immediately felt flushed and a little nervous. I'm glad she couldn't see me through the phone. I managed to work up the courage to ask her if she wanted to get something to eat. I was shocked when she said yes, but only if I would be willing to let her choose the restaurant, no questions asked.

"Of course," I thought. I wouldn't have cared if she wanted to go to a fast food joint. I just wanted to spend some time with her. After I hung up with her I called Quan and left him a message that something had come up, and that I would catch up with him later.

My heart was pounding when I arrived at Heaven's apartment. In the past she had kind of given me the cold shoulder, so I was little apprehensive about what to expect. "Well," I thought to myself, "I'm just going to walk up to that door, ring the bell and hope for the best."

I knocked twice and after what seemed like an eternity, Heaven opened the door. She looked drop dead gorgeous! She had her hair pinned up in a tight bun on top of her head, exposing her high cheekbones. This just proved to accentuate her beauty. Although she didn't need makeup, the little she was wearing highlighted her skin tone, and her face seemed to glow. She wore a casual dress, not too short, just enough to show off the butterfly tattoo on her leg. Her beauty mesmerized me, and I just stood there staring at her, totally speechless.

"Hi Ryan," Heaven said with this smile that could have melted ice. "Come on in."

Her voice jolted me out of my temporarily-comatose state and I walked through the door.

"Give me a second while I get my purse and keys," she said as she whisked off to the other room.

As I scanned the furniture and décor, I could tell right away that her apartment was the perfect reflection of her personality; clean, orderly and attractive, but not extravagant. As I glanced around the room I noticed a picture of Cousin Tonia and her on the table next to the sofa.

"Nice apartment, Heaven," I said as she walked back into the living room.

"Thanks," she said confidently. "My roommate and I do our best to make this our cozy little home away from home."

"Are you ready to go?" she asked with this clever-looking smile on her face.

"Yah," I said. "But first tell me where we're going."

"It's a secret," she said with a quick wink. "I promise you'll like it."

With that we headed out the door and got into Heaven's car. Since she was the one who knew our destination it only made sense that she should drive.

Market Street traffic was busier than usual. Friday night party goers, bar hoppers and tourists all converged on this main drag driving to their respective destinations. As we wove our way through traffic we exchanged small talk about school, work and our friends. I said nothing about Quan.

Heaven pulled up to this small building, which would have easily been missed if it hadn't been for the sign in front. It simply read "Laura's." In smaller print at the bottom of the sign it read, "Amateur Night." We drove to the back of the building and found a parking spot without any problem.

The hostess greeted us with a warm smile and escorted us to our table. The restaurant was unlike any that I had previously been to. The floors and tables were made from stained and treated wood that shone with a warm honey color. Small light bulbs glistened on the artificial trees that were strategically arranged around the perimeter of the room. And on a slightly raised platform a man was playing popular tunes on a piano to entertain the guests. The waitress and Heaven exchanged small talk and then took our order. I ordered a steak, medium rare, baked potato and a salad. Heaven followed suit.

"So tell me," I said to Heaven. "What's so special about this place and why did the waitress ask you if you were going to sing tonight?"

I felt like I was putting her on the spot, but she just looked at me with those sweet brown eyes of hers and said, "Well Ryan, Laura's is a very special place. The restaurant is alcohol-free and therefore caters to those who struggle with addictions, whether that's alcohol or some other substance. I don't think Laura would mind me telling you that she's a former alcoholic. After she gained her sobriety she decided to open up this place so that those who struggle with addictions would have a safe place to go for dinner and entertainment. At first people didn't think she stood a chance at being successful, considering the competition. But when she added the "Amateur Night" the place took off. People seem to be drawn to the casual atmosphere where you can enjoy a good meal and entertainment, even without having a drink. Kind cool, uh?"   "Yah," I nodded approvingly.

Heaven continued with her explanation, "When you mention non-alcoholic anything to guys at school, they make excuses and find somewhere else to go. That's why I kept it a secret. I wasn't sure what your reaction was going to be."

All I could think was, "I would have went just about anywhere with you girl, alcohol or not."

"So," I said. "You sing?"

"Yah a little," she said kind of sheepishly. "I'm not as good as my mother, but when I sing I do my best to please my Lord."

"Wow," I thought. A beautiful, talented woman who loves God, and she's spending time with me. But I was having a hard time processing why in the world she would take me to a non-alcoholic restaurant. Did she think I may have had a problem with drinking, or was she a former alcoholic? I was hoping we could get to the bottom of this before the evening was over.

It didn't take long for the waitress to bring our food. We talked and exchanged a few laughs as we ate our dinner, which was actually pretty good to my surprise. It wasn't very often that I loosened up enough around people to really be myself and enjoy the company. It was so easy to talk to her. I felt like I had known her all of my life.

Just as we were about to finish our dinner, the infamous Laura herself took the stage. We were seated right in the middle of the restaurant, so we had ideal seats for viewing the show. Laura was a natural, and had a commanding presence on stage. She asked if her patrons were having a good time and everyone responded with applause. Up until then we were being entertained by the piano player. It was pleasant background music and not so loud as to interfere with the conversations going on throughout the restaurant. I got the feeling that was about to change.

"Tonight friends, we have a special treat for you, Amateur night!" Laura said excitedly. "If you've got a special talent such as singing, dancing or acting that you're just itching to show off, this is your night. The first Friday of every month at Laura's we offer a $100 dollar prize for the winner of our talent contest. And you, the audience, will be the judges. So, who wants to be the first performer of the night?"

One man braved the crowd and made his way to the platform. He read some poetry that he had written. I appreciated his candor and creativity and evidently the crowd did also, politely applauding. The next contestant sang a song, also one that he had written. He was little off key, and his pitch was so high I believe he could have shattered glass. Man! I was glad when he got done. Heaven seemed to enjoy his song and smiled and clapped as if she were watching a performance in Carnegie Hall. "Oh well," I thought to myself, "to each his own, or should I say her own."   Laura came on stage, just in the nick of time in my opinion, and prompted the audience to consider laying down their inhibitions, throw caution to the wind and take their chances on stage. The crowd was scanning the audience to see who the next brave soul would be. I looked over at Heaven and said, "Your turn honey, let's see what you got."

"OK," she said. And with that she walked toward the stage as everyone clapped and encouraged her. Heaven grabbed the guitar that was propped up against the piano and made her way to the stool in the center of the platform. As she adjusted the mic she smiled that million dollar smile and said, "Thank you for the applause. Tonight I'll be singing 'Be the Change' by Britt Nicole."

Heaven's voice sounded as beautiful as her namesake. She sang with such conviction that it reminded me of the way Aunt Shirl sang the hymns at church. When Heaven finished her song, the reaction was fantastic. All the people simultaneously joined in a resounding applause and some even stood and whistled, cheering her on. The response was so overwhelming that I contemplated if I needed to rush to the stage and become her body guard.   "That was really cool," I thought to myself. Heaven returned to the table and I couldn't resist putting my arm around her and offering her my congratulations for a job well done.

"Stellar performance," I whispered in her ear as I gave her a tight squeeze.   "I had no idea you could sing like that, you're as good, or even better, than any professional I've heard," I said, convinced I was speaking the truth.

Heaven just smiled kind of unassumingly and said, "All the glory goes to my heavenly Father. He gave me this gift and I want to do my best to honor Him with it. Without Him, I wouldn't be where I am today, so I want to give Him all the credit. I don't mean to go Bible on you Ryan, this being our first date -- I mean if that's what you want to call this. But I can't help but quote, or should I say paraphrase James 1:17. It says that every good gift that we've been given the stewardship over, comes down from above from our heavenly Father. He never changes and there is no darkness in Him."

I didn't know whether to say Amen, alright or hallelujah. I had sense enough to know what she was saying was the truth, I just had never heard that God ultimately gets the glory for what He's given us. I thought it was all ours.

"Hey Heaven," I asked. "What's up with the song you sang, "Be the Change?"

"Glad you asked," she said. "Britt Nicole is one of my favorite female artists, although I have to admit I'm no match for her degree of talent. The words of that song encourage me to be a part of the catalyst that brings change into people's lives. Instead of accepting the discouraging things that life can sometimes throw at you, she inspires me to be a part of the solution and not the problem. Oftentimes people cave in under circumstances and confirm their doom by complaining to anyone that will listen. I choose to embrace the philosophy she has and make the best of everything through my attitude and actions. I want it to start with me. I want to be the light in the midst of someone's darkness, joy to those who are walking through sadness, healing to those who are hurting, help to the helpless, hope to the hopeless, love to the unlovable, and a friend to the friendless."

I just looked at her and thought, "What a great way to look at life."

I had lived such a sheltered life, at least as far as relationships were concerned, that I thought I was the only one who suffered the devastation I had. I was beginning to realize that there are no guarantees that we'll get through this life without pain, rejection and suffering. In fact, it's quite the contrary. It's not a matter of if we'll suffer, whether that be physical or emotional pain. Suffering is very much a part of the human condition. The point is, what will our attitude be about it? How will we choose to embrace, process and overcome it and then use those experiences to bless others?

As we were about to exit the restaurant Laura handed Heaven a check for $100. She won the talent contest, hands down. Laura also picked up the tab for our meal. What a great gesture. I had decided that I would definitely be back. I loved everything about this place.

Heaven and I continued our conversation and walked through the parking lot to the adjacent beach.

"So tell me, how did you wind up with such a beautiful name?" I asked. I just knew there had to be a story behind it.

"Well," Heaven said. "I was born with a heart murmur that affected my breathing, so consequently I was a very weak and sickly baby. The weeks following my birth the murmur gradually increased in size and the doctors told my mother that my chances for survival were slim. They had done everything they could, but my condition continued to decline. That's when my mother took things into her own hands and turned to 'the great physician.' She fasted and prayed for 30 days, bombarding heaven with her request for God to heal me and spare my life. And God did just that and sent her a miracle from heaven. The hole in my heart was miraculously healed without any surgical intervention. I was dubbed 'the miracle baby,' and hence, the name Heaven."

What a beautiful story, but she failed to mention a very important character, her father. "What about your dad? I asked. "Was he a part of your life at this time?"

She looked at me with an expression of disappointment and said, "My father left my mother when he found out she was pregnant with me. Neither one of us have heard from him since then. Over the years I considered looking for him, but my stepfather has always been there for my mom and me so I never pursued it."

I reached over to hold her hand and asked, "Do you ever wonder what could have been, I mean how your life could have been different had your dad chosen to be a part of your life?"

"No, not really. But on second thought maybe a little sometimes, you know, on birthdays and holidays," she admitted.

I felt like I needed to redirect the conversation so I asked her, "Heaven, so tell me what's the connection between you and Laura?"

"I used to work here part time for a little extra cash. I've always been pretty independent -- no handouts. I had to quit after I start taking on a full load at school, not to mention the Beta Club and my sorority. I like the atmosphere here. It feels safe, so I hang out here sometimes," she said.

"Ryan," she said shifting gears, "enough about me. It feels like I've been talking about myself all night. Tell me why a handsome young guy like you isn't involved with someone? I know quite a few of the girls at UNCW want to go out on a date with you."

"You're really my first official date, although I did meet this girl named Kim through my roommate Quan who introduced me to her. We were all at this party together a few weeks ago. Quan was with Kim's friend Courtney and eventually they left the party together. That was really an awkward moment for Kim and me. I guess they thought we would hook up, but as the night wore on we realized neither Quan nor Courtney could account for their whereabouts later that evening. Kim became really paranoid when Courtney didn't answer her phone, so I took her home. And when you came by the bakery that next day and informed us that another female student had been sexually assaulted off campus, my thoughts immediately went to Quan and Courtney."

Heaven then asked me, "Did you ever ask your roommate what happened that night?"

"Quan's kind of a mysterious guy," I replied. "I really can't figure him out. I asked him if Courtney made it home alright that night and he mumbled something about that she got what she deserved."

"What did he mean by that comment?" she asked.

"I guess he meant they did the nasty," I said with a smirk.

"Your roommate sounds scary," Heaven said with a look of concern. "Don't you think you need to report him?"

"I'm not 100 percent sure that's what happened, but it sure looks like it to me. I'll ask him about it the next time I see him. I don't want to file a false report," I said.

"OK, and oh yah, I want to thank for being so supportive in our fight to bring awareness to this sexual assault issue. We're not going to tolerate that, on campus, or anywhere else for that matter," she said very emphatically.

"No problem," I said with a smile. "I'm glad to help out any way I can. Call on me anytime."

We strolled along the moonlit beach, enjoying the scenery and one another's company.

Then Heather said, "It's so beautiful and peaceful out here. The moon's reflecting off the water and the only noise is the waves lapping against the shore." Then, out of nowhere she splashed a handful of water at me.

"I'm gonna get you for that," I said with a wide grin.

I reached down with both hands and got her good with a

huge splash of water. We both laughed and giggled at one another, just enjoying the fun. And then it happened. I reached over and touched her cheek and drew closer to her face and kissed her. It was a magical moment, but went far beyond the description my mother had given me many years ago. I was only hoping Heaven felt as wonderful as I did. Everything at that moment became so vivid, so alive, so exciting. The stars were lighting up the sky and my emotions were running wild. Here, in my arms, was the woman I had secretly admired from the first day I had laid eyes on her. Now we had embraced in our first kiss and it was the most wonderful feeling I had ever experienced in my life. I prayed in my heart that this moment would last forever.

A Time for Everything

"To everything there is a season, a time for every purpose under heaven."
-- Ecc. 3:1 NKJV

At the request of Terrance, Shirl, Tonia and I were meeting in the kitchen for an impromptu family conference. I guess Terrance had something he wanted to get off of his chest. Lately he looked as though something was bothering him and I had the feeling he was going to drop some kind of a bomb on us.

Terrance thanked us all for being there and without wasting any time got right to the point. Looking at Aunt Shirl he said, "Mom, I've been trying to find the right moment and the right way to talk to you about something that's been going on in my life. Every time I asked you for some of your time it seemed like you were busy with one problem or another. I guess what I have to say needs to be heard by everyone in this meeting -- so Ryan and Tonia, that's why I've asked you to be present."

Then he glanced my way and said, "Mom, it seems like since Ryan moved in you've been distracted with all the 'drama' of his situation. I know that he needs a certain amount of your attention, but mom, don't ignore us in the process of trying to help him."

Aunt Shirl sat there a little stunned, and me too, for that matter. I never thought I was taking away from the time and attention my cousins needed from their mother.

When she regained her composure she looked at him with the love of a mother in her eyes, took him by the hand and said, "I'm sorry son. I didn't realize I was ignoring you and I'm sorry that I made you feel like I was. Please tell me what's been on your mind."

"Well mom," Terrance began. "The 50th anniversary of the Blake Family Reunion is coming up soon and I would like to invite a friend of mine."

"OK son," Aunt Shirl said. "What's her name?"

I guess she somehow knew that this was a woman friend and not a man.

"Her name is Anna and we've been dating for some time now," Terrance said.

"So, why haven't I met her by now, and why on earth have you kept her away for so long?" asked Shirl.

Terrance had a perplexed expression on his face. We all could tell that something was bothering him.

Then, looking into his mother's eyes as though she were the only one in the room he said, "It's kind of complicated Ma. You see, she's white."

Shirl paused for a moment as if she were concentrating on how to word her next phrase.

"So tell me son," Shirl said. "How long have you been dating Anna?"

Terrance looked as though he had regained some of his confidence. He straightened up in his chair and shot a glance toward me. I think he was looking for my approval....kind of like he wanted someone in his corner for moral support.

Then turning toward Shirl he said, "I've been dating her for over two years now. I've thought about telling you a million times, but it never seemed like the right time. First one thing and then another," he said as he cut his eyes towards me.

I got the impression he was inferring that I had become a very present "distraction" in this family that somehow interferes with the quality of time Shirl has to divvy out to three sometimes very "needy" young adults.

Terrance continued his spiel to Aunt Shirl. "I know how you feel about us dating people who are outside of our race."

"Who told you that nonsense?" Shirl asked raising her voice.

"Nobody told me Ma," Terrance said. "I overheard you and Carol Gene talking about the Blake family bloodline not being tainted with any other race. So I took that to mean that our family has remained intact, all African American, no interracial relationships or biracial children."

"Son," Shirl said. "My business is where it is today because I have embraced a wide diversity of people by providing employment for them no matter what their race, religious beliefs or economic status. Also, I serve a cross section of our community, welcoming 'whosoever will' to come and patronize my business."

Terrance interjected, "The diversity of your employees and clientele has nothing to do with the Blake family heritage."

"True," Shirl replied. "Let me explain something to you and Tonia. And Ryan," she said as she looked in my direction, "I'd rather you hear this from me then from someone on the street. Kids, you see, the reason I never mentioned what I am about to say is because I didn't want you to grow up with a hateful heart towards people of another race. When Grandma Louise was a young woman, she worked as a maid for a wealthy white family named the Parker's. She cooked and cleaned for the family and tended to the children like they were her own, reading books to them and tucking them into bed. Mr. Parker had a thing for black women with big booties. One day while Mrs. Parker and the kids were out on a shopping trip, Mr. Parker made his move on Grandma Louise. She was in the kid's room making the beds and he came up from behind her and forced himself on her. He raped her, right there on one of his own kid's beds and told her if she said anything to anyone that he would have her killed."

"Well," she continued, "it didn't happen just that one time, but many other times after that. Then the inevitable happened. She wound up pregnant with his child. When she told him the news he punched her so hard she fell on the floor and then he proceeded to kick her in the stomach. She miscarried and consequently never told a soul what had happened. Back then black people were accused of any kind of trumped up false charge, and besides that she didn't want to lose her $2.50 a day wage. She was the sole provider for her three children. She also feared that Mrs. Parker would suspect her of high-stepping with her husband and blackball her from getting any other jobs in town."

Aunt Shirl continued to tell this horrific chapter in story of American history.

"Back in that era blacks in the South were hated, ridiculed, set on fire and lynched by malicious white gangs for having sex with white people, consensual or not. After that incident Mr. Parker, trying to find a way to get rid of Louise and sweep this all under the rug, accused Grandma of using an 'off limits' bathroom. Really all he was doing was creating a situation to get her fired, so they could hire some 'fresh meat.' Grandma kept her secret to herself for many, many years."

"Like you Ryan, she kept a diary. She chronicled the whole affair and told about the miscarriage, getting fired, and the day she contemplated throwing scolding hot water on his private parts for revenge. She had too much respect for Mrs. Parker to do such a thing. I guess she kept this secret bottled up inside of her for fear that no one would believe her, seeing there was no baby to prove that anything had actually happened."

All I could think was "WOW!" what a bomb to drop. I had studied American history, but they don't put this kind of a thing in textbooks. I had never realized that people could be so persecuted and taken advantage of.

Just then Terrance spoke up and said, "I'm sorry that anyone, never mind someone in our own family, had to be the victim of such abuse."

"Mom," he said. "I can see how there's bias and hatred between blacks and whites. I feel like I absolutely hate this man and I have never met him. Look at all she suffered she endured at the hands of this power-hungry, blood-thirsty vulture. He violated a young woman in the worst way a man could, murdered his own child and like a coward made it look like she was at fault and then fired her from her job."

Tonia was just sitting there with her mouth opened in horror and disbelief. As a young woman who was probably about the same age as Louise was when this happened, this story had an even greater impact on her than it did on Terrance and me.

She finally spoke and said, "That's the world we live in. And it's the world Grandma Louise lived in. People will hate you for the color of your skin, the texture of your hair, the person you choose to love and the neighborhood you choose to live in."

"I know," I said, "when I was in prison I saw firsthand the toll the corruption of our society has taken on its young men. And the penal system is just as corrupt. Most criminals are revolving inmates who repeatedly find themselves behind bars despite numerous previous stints in prison."

Just then Shirl interjected, this time directing her statement to Terrance. "So you see son, when you overheard my conversation about the Blake family, we have managed, through the grace of God and the grit of determination, to survive every unfair thing this world has managed to throw at us."

"Mamma," Terrance said. "I really hate what happened to Grandma Louise, but I need to know if there will be a problem if I bring Anna to our family reunion?"

"Of course not," Shirl replied. "She's more than welcome to attend and we'll treat her just like any other family member."

"OK," Terrance said. "I have something else to tell you. We, that is Anna and I, have a one-year-old son named Jaeden Henry Grason."

I looked at Aunt Shirl for her response and she just stared at Terrance. After what seemed like an eternity she spoke. "How could you keep this secret from me for a whole year?" she asked raising her voice. "I can accept you not telling me about Anna because girls come and go, but my own grandson! As your mother and Jaeden's grandmother, I deserve to know. Just what do you have to say for yourself young man?"

Terrance just hung his head in shame. Then he said. "Mama I thought....."

He was interrupted by Shirl who said, "Before you say anything else stupid, call Anna and tell her our family wants to meet her and your son. Black, white, green or yellow, that child is a part of this family and we will love and embrace him regardless of how he came into this world. Now grab your phone and get to dialing before I hit you upside your head!"

After the family meeting was over, Shirl asked me to go out and check the mail. I thought she needed a distraction from the drama and frankly I was glad to. I needed some fresh air after what just went down between her and Terrance. "This family certainly had its share of secrets," I thought to myself.

I grabbed the mail and noticed the letter on top was addressed to me. When I looked at the return address it was from Tank, my old Bunkie from Camp Penitude. I hadn't been keeping in touch with these guys like I should have so this was a real surprise. I tore the letter open and read:

Hey Homie,

Sitting here on my bunk and catching up on some letter writing. I've met this young lady on "Inmate Connection." You remember that program, don't you? It's a pen pal website for inmates to find friendship through written correspondence. We've been writing to one another for about four months now. She's a real cutie, works as a nurse and has a four-year-old son. The good news is she's planning on visiting me soon. You know how lonely it can get in here. I can't wait to meet her in person.

Everybody here is doing fine. D. Mac got into a scuffle on the basketball court and had to do some time in the hole. Other than that we're all just counting down the days when we can walk through those same gates that you did. Just know that you're never forgotten and I hope that you're staying out of trouble. Hope all is well with your family and they are giving you a fair shake. Stay strong and never look back because your best days are ahead of you.

Write back when you get a chance.

Your friend,

Tank

Granted, this letter wasn't as exciting news as a new baby in the family, but it meant a lot to me. I went up to my room, sat down at my desk and began to write a letter back to Tank and the guys in Camp Penitude.

Driven by Greed

"For the love of money is the root of all kinds of evil."
--1 Tim. 6:10 NKJV

Our basketball season didn't end very well. We lost pretty badly, 120 to 88, in the first round of playoffs to our division rival the Jayhawks. Quan, our point guard and leading scorer, missed the big game due to a one-game suspension he was slapped with because he missed a practice and was 30 minutes late for a mandatory team meeting. Coach Connors didn't take any flack when it came to bowing out of practice and team meetings without a legitimate excuse. And according to him there weren't many of those that he would accept either. You'd better have a doctor's note, a family emergency, or be laid up with an injury if you didn't want to face the wrath of Coach Connors.

In an effort to instill a sense of duty and responsibility in us, Coach also required that we maintain a 2.5 GPA, leave all the "drama" in the locker room, and participate in volunteer work in the community. His rationale was that we should be willing to give back to the people who consistently supported the athletic programs with their money and attendance at games. It just wasn't about basketball with him. He wanted us to understand what unity and integrity were all about and in doing so, also build our character.

Quan was definitely lacking in the qualities Coach Connors tried so hard to instill in us. He had absolutely no excuse for his irresponsible actions. He claimed the reason he didn't show up for practice was because he had a stomach virus. And he also said that he had lost track of time talking to his mom on the phone and wound up being late for practice. Even I thought those were pretty lame excuses; everyone else knew he was lying too.

Rumor had it that he was out riding his motorcycle with some guys over on Hill Crest, an area that's considered high risk for criminal activity. I was so disappointed about our loss to the Jayhawks that I confronted him about his selfish, immature behavior. He went on to tell me some nonsense about me not understanding the world he lived in and that he had more important things to worry about than the playoffs.

"What?" I thought. I was getting upset because I knew how much he loved the game. It was his life. He was always talking about hoping to one day play ball overseas or maybe even the possibility of making a run in the NBA draft. There was really something very wrong. I wanted to tell him about the conversation I had with Frankie Costner, but I promised him I wouldn't mention it to anyone. Too many possible repercussions. The timing had never seemed right to ask about that night with Courtney.

I had a gut feeling Quan's unexcused absences had a whole lot more to do with something other than a virus and losing track of time on the phone. I wanted to keep my distance.

I decided to hit the books that night to try to get my mind off of Quan and his antics. In the middle of my studies, the phone rang. What a welcome reprieve.

"Hello," I said.

"Hey Ryan, what cha up too?" Heaven asked.

Great, I was hoping she'd call! I didn't want to seem desperate, so I was glad she made the call instead of me.

"Not much," I replied. "I was just going over some of my economics homework. Believe me, you're a welcome voice if ever I heard one. I was starting to see double looking at all those numbers."

"Well," she said, "I'm glad you're in a good mood. I need someone to unload on."

"Ok hon, go ahead," I said.

"I just heard it from my mom that my biological father is in town and he had the audacity to ask her if she would arrange for me to meet him. I couldn't believe it," she said.

She continued with a tone of total disgust in her voice.

"Ryan, I consider this man an absolute disgrace to humanity for what he did to my mom and me. He walked away from us just when we needed him the most, and never looked back. Not one phone call for Christmas, birthdays, you name it. No child support to help out with school clothes, bills or whatever. This man never had the decency to own up to his responsibilities in any way at all. I have no use for him."

Man, she's really unloading. I didn't realize how broken she was over this; she's always so poised and in control. I guess this geyser of anger and bitterness needed to be vented, and I just happened to be the one she chose to spew it out on. I'm glad it was me and not a supposed girlfriend that might look at this as an opportunity for something juicy to gossip about.

Heaven continued with pouring out her soul to me.

"My stepdad took me in and loved me unconditionally, just like I was his own child. To tell you the truth Ryan, my mom and I are better off with my real dad out of the picture. I often wonder why God allowed this curse to be vexed upon my family."

I could hear the exasperation in her voice. I know she was frustrated and felt victimized by the betrayal and her powerlessness to do anything about it.

"Heaven, honey calm down," I said.

I could practically hear her heart beat through the phone.

"I'll calm down when he no longer wants to invade my life with his apologies and excuses. It's too little too late!" she said raising her voice.

"I know you're speaking from a wounded place...from a broken heart," I said trying to interject some logic into the conversation.

"Believe it or not," I said, "I've been in your shoes and I can't really say that I blame you for being angry. However, I do believe people can change and we have to make a choice to forgive and give them a second chance. Just look at my situation. I went from prison to college and getting my business degree."

"Prison!" Heaven exclaimed. "When were you in prison, and what in the world did you do? Tonia never said anything about prison to me. She told me you were coming to live with them because your parents died in a car accident."

"That's partially true," I said, when I realized what a bomb I had unintentionally dropped on her. I had done all I could in the past to dance around this chapter in my life and now I just spilled the beans, and big time. I had to think fast. There was no way I could, or even wanted to for that matter, explain my whole dysfunctional childhood while she was unloading all of her baggage on me.

"Heaven," I said hesitantly. "That part of my life is in the past. Believe me, I've paid my debt to society and am a reformed man. One day I'll tell you everything, I promise, but for now let's concentrate on your dilemma."

"Could it get any worse," she said. "I just can't believe our lives. Okay Ryan, this is more than I can handle right now. Could you fill me in on some of the details please?"

"The time I spent behind bars wasn't a total loss. I actually learned a lot about myself and how a tragedy like mine can be averted."

I was trying to deflect the conversation in such a way as to show her the positive side of an otherwise horrific situation while still encouraging her with what she was dealing with.

"You see," I continued. "While I was incarcerated I was privileged to have the most wonderful Christian psychiatric social worker a man could ask for. Her name was Dr. Grimes and she helped me confront and conquer my fears and also to come to terms with the horrific sin that caused my father to treat me like he did. He was very abusive towards me, both physically and emotionally. I came to realize that we were both victims who, because of our inner pain, wound up taking it out on the person we loved the most. Carrying around that burden was my self-imposed hell, one that was worse than the lonely, painful and sometimes frightening existence in prison. It was a process, and didn't happen overnight; but I had to make a choice to forgive him and myself, even though we both were guilty. There were some terrible things that happened to me at the hands of my father, and even though our experiences are somewhat different, Heaven, the results are the nonetheless the same....we're two broken people, full of potential, one that can only be realized through forgiveness. You'll have to deal with it or else you too will find yourself in a prison of anger, bitterness and resentment."

"I don't see how you forgive someone who is guilty," Heaven blurted out.

"Well, for starters," I said, "you need to confront the person who hurt you. My situation is unique, because my father is deceased. Dr. Grimes, through many therapy sessions, walked me through some techniques that helped me come to terms with my past fears and in doing so it allowed me to cope with and ultimately conquer the depression that had consumed me."

"Ryan, this conversation is getting way over my head and I need some big time clarification," Heaven said with confusion in her voice. "I can't understand how a person can forgive someone who's already in the grave. How in the world can that be possible?"

"Through counseling I realized that I had to visualize the offender, my dad, in my mind. It's kind of like resurrecting images from the past. Although some people choose to write letters to the perpetrator, or visit their graves, I had no choice but to choose the visualization technique. Once your mind has a clear image of that person you proceed to tell them what's on your heart and then process that information through your brain," I explained.

I'm sure this all sounded a bit surreal to Heaven.

I continued with my explanation: "Now I'm going to get a little technical, but stay with me and it will gradually make sense. Our memory functions somewhat similar to the way a computer operates. In order to retrieve a memory from our minds we have to reverse the process that stored it there. First significant events, people and experiences are encoded into our brains. Then that information is stored there, kind of like a memory bank. Certain environmental cues trigger that memory, but we can also consciously retrieve, process and eliminate those that are detrimental to our psychological and physical health. Still with me?" I asked.

"I think so," she said.

"Let me explain it like this; when I first met you I was so impressed that I recall exactly what you looked like, what you were wearing and what you said. I also remember all the details of our first date and the first time we kissed. Those memories are precious to me and will always have a special place in my heart, regardless of what happens to us. The memories with my dad weren't all bad, but in order to come to terms with the ones that were destroying me I had to rewind the images and make a choice to remove the damaging ones from my memory bank."

"Ryan, what happens if those ugly thoughts rear their heads and resurface?" Heaven asked.

"Well," I said, "I just make a choice to replace them with positive thoughts and like all unused information it eventually fades over time."

"Wonderful," she said, a smile in her voice. "I can really see you've been hitting those psychology books."

"Not really," I said. "I credit my healing to the Lord and for using Dr. Grimes as an instrument to bring deliverance to me."

Just then I heard some rustling from outside the front door, like someone was trying to force their way in.

"Heaven honey," I said as I got up off the couch, "Let me call you later. I hear some weird noises coming from behind the front door."

"Ok babe," she said. "Be careful. Call me back if you need to. If not I'll see you tomorrow."

I made my way to the door and asked, "Quan is that you?" Just then the noises abruptly stopped. "Hey Quan, man is that you out there?" I asked, this time with a louder voice.

I looked through the peep hole to try to see who it was. I couldn't see anyone, and as I unlatched the door it was forced open -- the impact almost knocked me over. Standing before me were two white guys and a black guy. I had never seen any of them before. Before I could really get a grip on what was happening one of the white guys pointed a gun to my face and said, "Where's your roomie Quan?"

"I, I, I....don't know," I said with my voice shaking from terror. "I haven't seen him since earlier today."

"You'd better not be lying," the same white guy said.

"Go check out the apartment," he ordered the other two thugs. "Bring him to me if you find the little coward."

As I stood there staring down the barrel of a sawed-off double-barreled shotgun all I could do was pray silently that Quan didn't come home unexpectedly and startle this guy. All of our nerves were on edge and I was sure it wouldn't take much for him to pull the trigger. My knees were shaking uncontrollably and I realized I had to go to the bathroom. I was in no position to ask for a favor so I just prayed under my breath for this whole nightmare to come to an end.

"Quan ain't here," the black guy said as he came out of the bedroom.

"You sure?" the gunman asked.

"Yah boss," he said. "We doubled checked everything; under the bed, the closet and the bathroom."

Just then the "boss" looked me square in the eye and pressed the barrel of the gun against my temple.

He said, "Pretty boy it would be an absolute shame if this gun went off and scattered your brains all over that wall for lying to me, now wouldn't it be? Now, I'm going to ask you one more time, where's Quan?"

I just stood there paralyzed; almost unable to even speak. Just then I realized something warm was running down my legs. I was so terrified that I was peeing all over myself.

One of the white guys threw his head back and laughing said, "Look boss, you scared the dude so much he peed his pants."

The "boss" laughed too, showing his gold fronts. He pressed the gun a little deeper into my skull and I blurted out, "Look man, I'm not lying. I don't know where Quan is."

I think the Lord heard my prayers because the gunman eased off of his death grip and lowered the gun.

"Boy, this is your lucky day," he said. "When you see that little scumbag tell him to get in touch with the boss. We've got some unfinished business to take care of. And don't even think about calling the police. Believe me, I'll find you, and it won't be pretty. You understand?"

With that they left the apartment and I quickly fastened the deadbolt lock.

"Oh God, thank you," was all I could say.

I tried to gather my composure as much as I could. I went into the bathroom, took a quick shower and changed clothes. I grabbed my phone and called Quan. I was unable to reach him, but left him a message to call me. I told him it was urgent.

I decided to try sleep on the couch and hope Quan showed soon. I lay down with my phone in one hand and a baseball bat in the other. I kept going over in my mind, who were these thugs that threatened my life and what could Quan have done to provoke something like this? After what seemed like an eternity I finally fell asleep.

I was awakened by the sound of keys rustling in the front door lock. I jumped to my feet, bat in hand ready to clobber the first person that stepped foot in that apartment.

"Is that you Quan?" I asked still groggy from the terrible bit of sleep I'd gotten.

"Yeah, it's me," he answered. "What's up with the bat?"

"Hey man, did you get the voicemail I left you?" I asked.

"I got your message, just don't knock my head off with that thing, okay," he said looking at the bat I still had gripped in my hand.

Putting the bat against the door and looking him straight in the eye I said in a raised voice, "Quan, three of your so-called friends paid you a visit last night. They were adamant about talking to you about something and even thought I knew your whereabouts. One of them they called 'Boss' had a gun pointed to my head the whole time they were here, while the other two thugs tore the place apart looking for you. He told me not to go to the police or, in his words, 'it wouldn't be pretty.' What the heck's going on man? What have you gotten yourself mixed up with?"

"Ryan, I'm sorry you had to go through that last night," Quan said apologetically. "The Rarecias Brothers gang is bad news and their threats are not to be taken lightly. Whatever you do, don't even think about going to the police or this could get a lot worse."

"Wait a minute," I said. "Let me get this straight. These guys barge into our apartment, hold a gun to my head, ransack the place looking for you and you want me to act like nothing happened? Have you lost your mind or what? Now tell me what they were doing here and why they were looking for you, and don't even think about lying to me."

Quan had this distraught look on his face like he'd been caught red handed with something.

Then he blurted out, "I owe them $10,000 dollars. I lost it gambling."

"OK back up a minute," I said as I shook my head in disbelief. "Some of the pieces of this puzzle are missing, and the rest of them don't fit together. First, why do you owe them $10,000 dollars and when did you start gambling?"

"Okay Ryan," he said. "I'm going to give it to you straight. For the past year I've been supplying the campus junkies with the drug of their choice. I was pushing anything from pot to pills and even a little coke for the rich kids. I know it's terrible, but the money I made I sent home to help with my dad's medical care. He's got brain cancer and the insurance just doesn't cover all the expenses...chemo, radiation, medications and doctors' visits. I feel like I owe my parents. They've sacrificed so much for me, it's the least I can do for them. I send it to them via a family friend so there are no questions asked. And as far as the gambling goes, I grew up watching my dad hustle any way he could. He was no stranger to gambling. Many a night he'd be out at the local pool hall, and if he wasn't there, you could find him in our basement hosting card games. It was as normal to us as going to church was for the rest of our neighbors."

"Quan, sorry about your dad and all, but could you not think of a better way to help your parents than selling drugs? Come on man, give me a break."

"I know, I know," he said, "I lost all that money on a bet racing my motorcycle up on Hill Crest. There was this high roller flaunting his cash around, just daring me to take him on. I thought I could beat him and double my money, but he edged out a win by a half a bike. It was real stupid of me to take that challenge, knowing I was betting with the Rarecias Brother's money. They fronted me a 'package' and when I didn't make my payment on time they came looking for me. I've been trying to avoid them until I can get the money together."

"Quan, I'm not going to keep playing this game of Russian roulette with you. Those guys who busted in are serious about their money and drugs. You jeopardized my safety last night, and God only knows what those guys are capable of. What if they beat me up or kidnapped me? They wouldn't think twice about killing anyone who got in their way just to make a statement."

Quan just hung his head in shame and nodded in agreement.

"Well look," I said. "We can't act like this never happened, we've got to do something. Since we can't go to the police I've at least got to let my Aunt Shirl know what's going on. I know she'll help us out. These guys want their money and they'll stop at nothing to get it. It's not safe here -- we've got to leave, my friend."

Quan's face lit up like a lightbulb with that glimmer of hope. Just the suggestion that my family could be instrumental in starting the long road back to a normal life, whatever that is, was all the incentive he needed to spring into action.

"Ok Ryan that's fine," he replied as he placed his arm around my shoulder. "Before we get ready to go I want to apologize for jeopardizing your safety. You've been nothing but a true friend to me the whole time I've known you."

He swallowed hard, looked me in the eye and said, "Please forgive me. You, of all people, didn't deserve that."

"I forgive you," I said realizing how many times in my life the same grace had been extended to me.

An Unexpected, Undeserved Gift

"Kindness is a language which the deaf can hear and the blind can see."
--Mark Twain

It was morning by the time Quan and I found ourselves in Aunt Shirl's living room. To tell you the truth, neither one of us knew what to expect, we just knew there was nowhere and no one else to turn to. As I explained the dilemma Quan had gotten himself into, I could tell by the look on Shirl's face that she was both amazed and disillusioned by the story. As I struggled to see things from her perspective, I could only imagine the difficulty she was having trying to comprehend how her nephew could have gotten tangled up with an admitted drug dealer and gambler, one who evidently didn't think twice about jeopardizing his safety -- not to mention the safety of all the people he sold drugs to.

As I continued to explain all the sordid details I could see Aunt Shirl scooting herself to the edge of her chair and staring at Quan with such a look of disappointment, one that I hoped she would never have the occasion to look at me with. I'm sure Shirl had heard her share of "horror stories," raising two kids of her own, with the majority of those years having raised them as a single mother.

Quan, by society's standards, was the scum of the earth. Even though he had parents who obviously cared about him, he had somehow fallen through the cracks and wound up like so many young men, criminals and victims of their own poor judgment. All of this insanity was fueled by the insatiable appetites of lust and greed. Although Quan's intentions were somewhat noble, selling drugs so he could help support his parents who were dealing with the financial burden of overwhelming medical bills, he nonetheless had chosen to do so not only by breaking the law, but by endangering the well-being of everyone who was close to him. Talk about not thinking things through! Although this "business venture" may have initially proven to be a lucrative one, the risks far outweighed the benefits.

As I was contemplating all of this in my mind, Aunt Shirl arose from her chair and walked over to where Quan was sitting, his head hung low in utter disgrace. I really wasn't sure if she was going to chew him out or kick him out. But to my amazement, and I'm sure to the utter shock of Quan, she reached her arms out to him and gave him a warm, loving hug, one that can only come from the heart of a mother. As she held him in her arms she said, "Son, you've really gotten yourself into one more mess and we've got to figure out a way to get you out of it."

Quan began to sob as he came to the realization of just how much was at stake because of his foolish choices. I think he was also overwhelmed with the undeserved love that was extended to him, when his expectation was to be the recipient of quite the opposite reaction. He apologized repeatedly for his actions and for unintentionally endangering so many people, especially his best and only friend.

After using up half a box of Kleenex, Shirl was eventually able to initiate a conversation between them. "Who are these thugs anyways?" she asked. "Did you say they call themselves the Rarecias brothers...or something like that?"

Quan, finally lifting his head and wiping his nose, responded, "I met them at a party through a mutual friend, a guy name Chicharito. He told me they were in town on business. When I asked him what kind of business he said pharmaceutical sales and distribution. I knew exactly what he meant by that statement and I asked him what they were doing in the Wilmington area. He told me they were looking to expand their base operation from the Florida Keys to North Carolina. That information really piqued my interest."

"You see Shirl," Quan continued, "for the past year I've been pedaling small amounts of marijuana to make a little money. My dad has cancer and the medical bills are more than my parents can afford and they were about to lose their house. So I've been sending them money through a family friend so as not to arise any suspicion. I figured I could up the ante if I got hooked in with the Rarecias brothers, using Chicharito as the middle man. He supplied me with all the drugs I needed based on the demand from the students on campus. Since I was fronted the drugs, I made my money on the back end, kind of like a loan from the bank. As I've already told Ryan, my intention was to pay the Rarecias brothers on time, but greed in the form of a bet on a motorcycle race, messed up my plans...and big time."

"Okay Quan," Shirl said. "I think I'm following you so far and I can see how this is going from bad to worse. Just give me the details of what actually happened so I can make some sense of this whole thing."

"OK, OK," Quan said. "Well anyway, a couple of weeks ago I ran into these street brawlers up on Crest Hill. They were ranting and raving about how fast their motorcycles were and dared anyone to race them, laying $5,000 on the line as bait for a bet. Since there were two of them I thought I could easily beat them both and double my money. I used the money I owed the Rarecias brothers and laid it all on the line. Well, the race didn't go as I expected and I was beat out by half a tire length. So I forfeited out $10,000 dollars that day, money that wasn't even mine. The irony of it all is that I was supposed to meet Chicharito that night to pay him what I owed him. So I'm trying to avoid him, at least until I find someone who is willing to buy my motorcycle."

Just then Aunt Shirl interrupted him and said, "Those guys are out for blood. They probably think you stole the drugs they fronted you when you didn't show up with their money. The logical explanation would be to go to the police, but this is anything but a logical situation. If we do that you'll wind up getting arrested, it won't look good for my nephew her, and worse, the Rarecias brothers will eventually kill you for ratting them out.

It looks like your only option is to pay them off. I know neither you nor your parents have that kind of money, but I do."

Quan and I looked at her with total disbelief. Was she offering to pay off the debt of a drug dealer, one that he admittedly gambled away?

Before we could come to terms with what seemingly was the greatest act of grace since the cross, Shirl blurted out, "Okay Quan, this is what I'm going to do, and even though it goes against my better judgment, I see no other solution to this problem. I'll loan you the money to pay these guys off and get them off your back. But this loan is based on three very strict stipulations. First, you have to stop selling drugs. Second, you have to call your parents and tell them the whole story. If you want to help them out financially you need to get a part time job. I can always use some extra help at the shop."

"Thirdly young man," Shirl said as she pointed her finger at Quan, "after you graduate from school and start working, I fully expect you to pay me back. You don't have to do it all at once, just so you understand that this is not a hand out. And you'd better not be lying to me about your father having cancer. I'll beat you up myself, then, I promise."

None of us were sure how, or even if, we could pull this off, but we were going for it. This wasn't totally legal, but to involve the police at this point would complicate things, to say the least. We may be unwittingly inviting them into this after all. All we could do was pray that this worked out for the best for everyone concerned, especially Quan.

I slipped out of the living room, remembering I needed to return a text from Heaven from the previous night. She was concerned about me, only knowing in part and thereby speculating on what I had gone through at the apartment the night before. I waited to call her back realizing that she would have been hysterical and immediately would have called the police. Heaven is very pro-active when it comes to any kind of violence, especially on campus. She firmly believes it is her mission to see that UNCW is a safe haven for students, a place where they can obtain an education, free from the fear of being violated in some way by deranged lunatics.

I called her from the kitchen, giving myself a safe distance from Aunt Shirl and Quan. I tried as best I could, relaying as much detail as possible, to explain the dilemma Quan had gotten himself into. She was not as forgiving and gracious as Aunt Shirl had been, not even close. She was totally convinced that there was enough evidence to have Quan expelled from school and banned from campus for selling drugs. Of course, from a legal standpoint she was right, and he deserved jail time. But I was hoping for a different reaction. She also directed her accusations towards me since I would not turn this over to the campus police, laying the burden of guilt on me for supposedly trying to cover up for him.

"Ryan," she said. "I can't believe you're asking me to compromise everything I've worked so hard to accomplish this past year. Quan deserves everything he's got coming to him. Can't you see that he's using you to help him get out of the mess he's gotten himself into? Everyone on campus knows he's up to no good and to tell you the truth I'm surprised he made it this long without already getting arrested."

Then she went Bible on me. "You know it's written in the Good Book, 'Sow bad seed and bad things will happen.' What did he expect, and what in the world are you thinking?" she asked furiously. "Can't you see that everything has finally caught up with him, and it's time for him to pay his dues? I think it's more than obvious what we need to do -- take this to the authorities before anything worse happens," she exasperated.

"Heaven, honey please. You don't understand how scared I am. Those thugs pointed a gun to my head and warned me if I went to the police that they'd find me and it wouldn't be pretty. Don't you see what's at stake here? The solution to this problem is not as black and white as it appears. You've got my safety to take into consideration now!"

I was wondering if she was even listening to me. I know the whole thing must have sounded like the storyline in a movie to her, but this wasn't a movie, this was reality and we had to think fast and think smart.

"Listen Heaven," I said. "My Aunt Shirl agreed to loan Quan the money he owes these guys and hopefully they'll get off his back, and mine too. I just don't think you understand what kind of people we're dealing with and as we see it there's no other alternative. Please try to take the whole situation into consideration, and see it from our perspective. I chose to tell you the truth because I thought you deserved it."

I was hoping that illogical logic made sense to her.

"Ryan," she said. "I've got a bad feeling about this. I hope you all know what you're doing."

We were both silent for a moment.

"Listen," she said with a sigh. "I've got something important I've got to take care of this morning, so I'm going to have to cut this call short."

"Okay babe," I said. "Catch up with you later. Bye."

Quan had evidently been on the phone with his parents because when I walked back into the living room he looked like he'd been crying. Shirl was nowhere in sight. I guess she went to the bank to withdraw the money she was going to loan him.

"Everything okay man?" I asked.

"Not really," Quan said lifting his head and wiping his eyes. "I called my mom and she was absolutely furious with me for the stupid things I've gotten myself involved with, regardless of my intentions. She was so hysterical at one point that Shirl got on the phone and tried to calm her down, reassuring her that she was going to loan me the money I owed these guys. My mom insisted I go to the police before things got any worse. I told her that was a bad idea, considering they had already threatened your life. She also wants me to transfer schools so that I can be closer to home."

"Man, what a mess," I thought.

Trying to see if there was any hope for this situation I asked, "What did your dad say?"

"I didn't even get a chance to talk to him," he said. "He was upstairs resting and I didn't want to make things any worse for him. I just thought it would be best for my mom to tell him."

"Let's just hope everything works out," I said as I wrapped my arm around his shoulder.

Shirl returned from the bank with a fresh stack of one hundred dollar bills, wrapped in a brown paper band labeled "$10,000." Not wanting to waste any more time, Shirl instructed Quan to take the money to the people he owed it to. She was very emphatic when she told him that if she didn't hear from him within the hour that she was definitely going to the police, no exceptions. I offered to ride along with him in case anything went wrong, but he said that he could handle this himself.

I gave Quan my car keys and as he walked out the door Shirl lifted her head in prayer, realizing just how dangerous this could be. She asked the Lord, "Oh Lord, I hope we made the right decision. Please watch over this young man and don't let any harm come to him."

That was all the drama I could take. All the stress of the last couple of days had caught up with me, so I told Aunt Shirl I was going upstairs to try to rest my eyes some until we heard back from Quan. When I got to my room I noticed a letter addressed to me from Dr. Grimes lying on my pillow. It had been over a year and a half since I had heard from this woman who had had such a powerful impact on my life.

I couldn't wait to open the letter and see what she had to say.

Dear Ryan,

I hope all is well with you and you are continuing on your pathway to recovery. I was sifting through some of my files and came across yours, so I thought I would drop you a line. The last time we spoke you were at odds as to whether or not you should move to Wilmington, NC to live with your father's sister. I know that was a tough decision for you, and I pray that it's working out for you.

Ryan, you are an exceptional young man who has triumphed over so many insurmountable odds. As a professional counselor and a psychiatric social worker, it's very rewarding to me to know that my input has had an impact on my patient's lives. The difference I made in your life I want you to re-invest into the lives of others. In doing so, you will help them to continue on a quest of discovery and deliverance from the hidden fears that stifle the truth of who they really are.

We made so much progress while you were here at Camp Penitude. It is my hope that you are continuing to add value to your life so that you will be able to significantly impact the lives of others. Please send me an update on what you've accomplished since the last time I've heard from you. It was good to hear that you successfully completed your nine months of probation.

If you ever lose sight of who you are and what great things you are capable of, don't hesitate to call me. Stay encouraged and keep living a life of integrity, showing others what it looks like to be an overcomer in this complicated world.

Yours Truly,
Sharon B. Grimes
Psychiatric Social Worker

Camp Penitude

What a blessing to hear from Dr. Grimes. This letter couldn't have come at a better time.

Truth or Consequences

"When you choose your behavior, you choose your consequences."
--Dr. Phil

Dr. Grimes' letter gave me some much needed relief from the whole "Quan dilemma." I had run all the "what ifs" through my mind a million times over. What might happen to Quan at the hands of these thugs? What if Heaven went "AWOL" on me and called the cops? After tossing and turning on my bed like a rag doll in a washing machine for what seemed like an eternity, I was so exasperated that I gave up on trying to get sleep. I threw a shirt on and walked downstairs to see if there'd been any word from Quan.

Aunt Shirl was walking back and forth, phone in hand, marking a groove in the living room carpet with her continued, incessant pacing. She was really making me nervous, adding to my already frazzled nerves. It had been well over an hour since Quan left with the payoff and Shirl and I were both thinking the worse. Our imaginations were running wild with the possibilities of what these criminals could be capable of. Had we really done the right thing by not getting the police involved?

"Oh Lord Ryan," Shirl said with a look of anguish on her face. "I'm not feeling very good about this. Quan should have already called. We have no idea where he is or what might have happened to him. Maybe we should call the police. I can't believe I agreed to this scheme you and Quan dreamed up."

"What do you mean, scheme?" I asked defensively. "This 'scheme' was something you suggested and we all agreed to. There was no other choice in the matter considering who we were dealing with. If we had gotten the police involved, all of our lives would have been in jeopardy, maybe even yours. These guys will stop at nothing to get what they want," I said.

I thought we had settled all of this before Quan left. Now that things seem to be backfiring.

"I'm just saying Ryan, if something terrible happens to him, his blood will be on our hands," Shirl said still gripping the phone in anticipation.

Just then her phone rang. We both looked at each other with a look of fear and relief, if that's possible. It faded to a look of disappointment when she saw the caller I.D. and realized that it was Pastor Taylor. Maybe this was God's way of intervening, but Shirl evidently didn't think so. People say your true colors come through when you're under pressure. Shirl was scared, scared for what might have happened to Quan and scared of what people, especially her Pastor, might think if she explained the whole mess.

"Hello Pastor," Shirl said in an upbeat voice.

"Oh no Pastor, all is well," she said a little hesitantly. "I'm sorry I missed our meeting. It totally slipped my mind. I got distracted talking to my nephew, please forgive me."

After a moment Shirl said, "Ok Pastor, thanks for being so understanding, I'll tell him. Bye."

"Pastor Taylor said to tell you hello," Shirl said.

I could tell by the look on her face that she was just about to the point where she was going to lose it. I was surprised that she held her composure as well as she did while she was on the phone. If things turned south and we found ourselves in a bigger mess than we were already in, she might need the support of her church and Pastor.

As I walked out of the living room I looked down at my phone as it rang and saw "Restricted" on the screen. "I wondered who that could be," I thought?

"Hello," I said.

"I'd like to speak with Ryan Blake," the man's voice on the other end of the line said.

"Speaking," I said.

"We found a car registered to you parked near an abandoned building on the west side of town with the driver's side window smashed. A man, whom we identified as Quan Jeffery and the suspected driver, was laying on the ground in a pool of his own blood, barely conscious, an apparent victim of a beating. Do you know anything about this?" he asked.

A thousand thoughts ran through my mind. What was I going to say? If I said yes I would possible incriminate myself, and if I said no I would be lying to the police. Our worst nightmare had come to pass. Quan's life was lying in the balance and though we had tried so hard to avoid disclosing this to the police, they were the very ones who were ultimately saving his life. Talk about irony!

"Well sir," I said. "Quan's my friend and I did let him borrow my car."

"Ok," he said. "We'll talk about this in more detail later. We've transported him to County Hospital if you'd like to see him."

"Ok thank you sir," I said as I hung up the phone.

I hurried back into the living room to deliver the bad news to Shirl.

"I just got a call from the police. Quan got beat up really bad and he's at the hospital." She looked at me and dropped the glass of water that was in her hand, spilling it all over the carpet. She couldn't catch her breath, couldn't even force her lungs to draw half a mouthful of air. She just closed her eyes and wrung her hands and looked upward, like she was going to pray.

"Auntie….Auntie, are you alright?"

She just nodded without saying a word.

"Come on Aunt Shirl, we've got to get to the hospital," I said taking her by the hand. "Let me drive," I said.

We both got in the car and headed to the hospital. The 30 minute ride to the hospital seemed to take forever. Shirl was in deep thought as I darted in and out of traffic, barely abiding by the rules of the road. Again, all the "what ifs" were racing around my mind. I wondered how this could have happened when he had the money they were looking for. Did they even get the money, or did they beat people up first and ask questions later? I really didn't know what to think. Obviously we were dealing with people who weren't rational and wanted to make a statement no matter what the circumstances.

I also reconsidered what Heaven had said about going to the police. Was I being rash and unreasonable, just as I had accused her of being? I thought about what Frankie Costner had said to me that night in the parking lot. Could I have been the one to prevent all of this? I just sunk into a sense of hopelessness and confusion. People say that hindsight is 20/20 vision. If I had to do it all over again I think I would have handled things a little differently, but it was too late for that. We were now on the way to the hospital, hoping to get there before my friend died.

We arrived at the hospital and made our way to the emergency department. As we walked up to the nurses' station we noticed a police officer standing there talking with the charge nurse. I hoped he wouldn't have any questions for us, at least not right now.

We both, acting like he wasn't there, bypassed him completely and made a beeline for the nurse.

"Do you have a patient by the name of Quan Jeffery?" Shirl asked.

The policeman then interjected, "My name is Officer Cheek. Are you related to Mr. Jeffrey?"

"No," Shirl stated. "My nephew, Ryan Blake, is his college roommate and I'm a concerned friend."

"Well Mr. Blake," Officer Cheek said. "I spoke with you over the phone about the crime scene my partner and I happened upon while on a routine patrol. Whoever beat your friend left him there to die. If we hadn't found him when we did it's quite possible we would be conducting a murder investigation right now. Robbery could have been a possible motive but at this point everything is pure speculation pending an investigation. Your friend is the only eyewitness we have at this point, so we're hoping we can get a good description of the perpetrators…that is if he wakes up. We'd like to contact his family. Do you have a phone number we could use to call his parents?"

"Yes," Shirl interjected. "I have it right here in my phone."

"Okay, thank you," he said as he wrote the number down and handed it to his partner.

I realized that Shirl was trying to protect me and keep me from saying anything that would unknowingly incriminate me. I had a tendency to speak before I thought. Even though I was 19 years old she still felt like I was her responsibility and I had to admit it felt good that someone was willing to take a stand in my defense.

"We're just looking for answers ma'am," Officer Cheek said reassuringly. "So if you or your nephew know anything that would aid us in this investigation, we need to be made aware of it."

Shirl nodded and took a step backward, careful to still remain within earshot of the conversation. I noticed out of the corner of my eye that Officer Cheek's partner had approached Shirl and tapped her on the shoulder. Maybe this was the break, the diversion, I had been hoping for. I really wasn't sure what to tell the police. It scared me to tell the truth and it scared me not to.

Now both Officer Cheek and I were riveted on what his partner had to say to Aunt Shirl.

"Ma'am," he said. "I spoke with Mrs. Jeffrey, Quan's mother, and she requested that you call her as soon as possible. She also told me that you loaned her son some money to pay off some drug dealers. Is that true?" he asked with a furrowed brow.

Shirl turned to me, I guess in an effort to gain some moral support. Now we both were on the spot with literally no way of escape. One of us had to tell the truth and let the chips fall where they may. We had to come to terms with what we had tried so hard to avoid. The same people we thought would jeopardize our safety, that being the police, were the same ones who now held our fate in their hands.

Shirl spoke up and told the officer questioning her all the sordid details of the whole story. She held nothing back, hoping they would be able to see things from our perspective. Surely a situation like this one, with so much compassion and goodwill, couldn't be illegal...or could it?

Just then a doctor approached us and asked if we were any relation to Quan. We told him we were close friends and that his family had been notified of his condition, although they were from out of town. The doctor escorted us to a private room and proceeded to tell us the extent of Quan's injuries.

"We've taken him to the ICU and are currently monitoring his vital signs. What we're most concerned about is the swelling on his brain. We're giving him I.V. infused meds and have put him into a medically induced coma in the hopes that the swelling will go down. He also has two broken ribs, a fractured jaw, and numerous cuts and contusions to his face. At this point we give him about a 50 per cent chance of pulling through. The next 48 hours are crucial to his survival and recovery. Sorry to be the bearer of such bad news, but I've seen a lot worse. We can be thankful these officers came upon him when they did."

"Thank you doctor," Shirl said shaking his hand. "Can we see him?"

"Let's wait until his next of kin arrives," the doctor said reassuringly.

As we stood there trying to absorb all of this information and wrap our minds around what we may have unintentionally caused, Officer Cheek interjected a remark to Aunt Shirl.

He said, "Ma'am, I want to put you and your nephew at ease concerning the possibility of charges being filed against you as accessories to this crime. It's not against the law to loan someone money, we just don't understand why we weren't contacted. I know you were afraid of these guys, and rightly so, but we could have set up a decoy, and quite possibly have made an arrest. Too late for that now."

Shirl and I looked at each other and simultaneously exhaled a huge sigh of relief.

Since Quan had no other family in the immediate area, Shirl agreed to spend the night at the hospital. She was way too nervous to drive anyway. Quan's mother was scheduled to arrive the following morning. Shirl had graciously agreed to pay for her air fare.

Two officers had been assigned to Quan's room, not only for his protection, but in the event he regained consciousness they wanted to be available to obtain a description of the guys who beat him up. I gave them a brief description of the thugs who barged into the apartment a couple of nights ago and threatened me. Why should I fear the police? At this point they were the only ones who could help us. I still wanted justice for my friend and this was the only way it would be possible.

Shirl called Terrance and let him know that she wouldn't be home that night because she would be spending the night at the hospital, standing in for a mother who could not be there for her son.

"Look here young man, don't let me hear you say that again," I heard her say to Terrance.

Boy, I would love to have heard his reaction to his mom's latest escapades. All this drama certainly wasn't helping my relationship with my cousin. One more consequence of this whole mess!

"Ryan didn't know anything about his roommate being involved in drugs. He fell victim to Quan's mess through no fault of his own. So don't let me hear another negative word from you about your kin. Is that understood? I'll see you in the morning."

Shirl ended the call kind of abruptly and turned towards me. I was perched up against the wall trying to absorb all the events of the past couple of hours. She motioned with her hand for me to come and sit beside her on the couch. I nudged close to her and rested my head on her shoulder.

"Are you alright?" she whispered softly.

"Yeah, I'm fine," I said. "I'm just praying that Quan pulls through this."

"Me too baby, me too," she said as she rubbed my weary head.

A Desperate Plea

"Lord, hear my voice: let your ears be attentive to the voice of my supplications."
--Psalm 130:2 NKJV

Quan's mother Katherine, arrived at the Wilmington International Airport the following morning. I had driven to the airport to pick her up, not quite sure I would recognize her. Without her introducing herself to me, I knew immediately who she was. She was a petite woman who had the same skin tone and facial features as Quan, even down to the mole both of them had on their faces. Sometimes you can just tell when people are kin to one another.

Surprisingly her demeanor was rather upbeat, considering she had a son in ICU and a husband at home battling brain cancer. Most people in this situation would be anxious, to say the least, but there was an inner strength that graced her face, one that emanated from deep within her soul. Years ago I heard my mother referring to this quiet confidence as "fire power." It's a knowing, that regardless of how challenging and hopeless something may seem, there's Someone greater, the Comforter, from Whom we can draw the hope and resiliency to rise above the prevailing circumstance. The few times my mother talked to me about the Lord she told me that every believer, upon acceptance of Jesus Christ as Savior, receives a measure of faith and a small portion, or seed, of the character of God.

As a small boy I was captivated by the fact that I could possess a supernatural strength just by calling on the name of Jesus. As a young adult I now realized it does require an act of my faith, but as a little kid it was no different than the power the superhero figures I played with possessed. Little did I know then that there were dark satanic forces that one day I would have to confront in the form of injustice, pain and suffering...to mention a few. Life had proven to be a lot more complex than the imaginary power of my superheroes. I was still coming to terms with my faith, embracing it at one moment and questioning it the next.

Mrs. Jeffrey walked towards me humming that old Gospel tune, "Pass Me Not O Gentle Savior." It brought back the memory of the other verses in that song: "Hear my humble cry, while on others Thou art calling, do not pass me by."

When I looked at her and acknowledged that I recognized the tune I asked her, "Would you by chance be Quan's mother?"

She answered, "Yes I am son. And you must be Ryan, Quan's friend. And that song I'm humming is an old Gospel tune my mother taught me to sing when I really needed the Lord to intervene. Right now I'm fully expecting Him to lift the shadow of death from my son's life."

"Yes ma'am," I said as I extended my hand towards hers.

I helped her with her luggage and led her to Shirl's car. The ride to the hospital was one of tension mixed with added comments of pleasantries and small talk.

When we arrived at the hospital Aunt Shirl looked physically drained and emotionally exhausted. She had spent the last 16 hours at the hospital, tormented by guilt blaming herself for what had happened. I had seen that look of exasperation on her face before -- at my sentencing hearing. As then, she sat in the seat of uncertainty, waiting for the outcome. Well hopefully, as with my life, this sense of hopelessness would be short lived and Quan's life would mirror the same success story that I hoped I was in the process of becoming.

The two mothers shared a warm embrace and Katherine thanked Shirl for paying for her air fare. Katherine, anxious to hear an update on Quan's prognosis, immediately walked to the nurse's station, introduced herself and requested to see Quan's doctor.

Within a few minutes Dr. Hunter, a tall slender man, walked through the double doors of the ICU and walked over to Katherine.

"Hello," he said extending his right hand. "I'm Dr. Hunter. And you must be Quan's mother, Mrs. Jeffrey."

"Yes I am doctor," she said. "I was hoping you could tell me some good news about my son."

"Let's step into the patients' lounge," he said motioning to the door on his left, "where we can talk with you and your friends a little more privately."

"Well," Dr. Hunter said to Katherine as we were all seated together, "as I told you previously over the phone his injuries are quite severe. If the swelling has not receded by morning we'll have to do surgery to drain the blood on his brain."

Quan's mother had a look of dread on her face and a tear rolled down her cheek. She quickly gathered her composure and asked, "Can I see my son?"

Out of the corner of my eye I saw Shirl take her by the hand just to let her know we were there for her. Again I saw the tears well up in Katherine's eyes and although she struggled to hold them back the tears started to roll down her face. It was then that Shirl embraced her and let her cry on her shoulder. I even found myself getting a little teary eyed over the grave news and Katherine's broken heart.

As we entered the ICU the two officers assigned to the case were at their post guarding Quan's room. They reminded me of two watchdogs guarding their owner's property. It was a tense moment, but we managed to get Katherine into the room without her getting too emotional. As we entered the room and got closer to the bed, we realized it was one thing to hear a doctor's description of someone's injuries, but quite another to see someone you love laying in a bed totally helpless, covered in bandages and hooked up to monitors and IVs. All around him the machines beeped, the IVs pumped and the respirator wheezed. Quan's face was badly bruised and swollen beyond recognition, but the sounds of the life support systems and the expansions and contractions of his chest gave us all some semblance of hope.

"Hey baby," Katherine said stroking Quan's hand as she spoke quietly into his ear. "This is momma. If you can hear me honey, your father sends his love and is praying for a speedy recovery. The doctor says you've really got to put up a fight if you want to come through this. Daddy and I need you at home with us. We'll figure out how to handle this situation together, just keep fighting and get your strength back. I love you baby."

Katherine gently kissed him on the forehead and began humming the same Gospel song she was humming when I picked her up at the airport. "Pass me not O gentle Savior...."

Aunt Shirl was slumped over the foot of Quan's bed praying, "Oh Lord, I know you have the power to heal this young man. I ask you, in the name of Jesus that the swelling in his brain recedes by morning. I believe you will not put any more upon your children than they can bear and with each testing you give us a way of escape. Katherine is bearing a heavy load right now. Help her cast her care upon You and You will sustain her. I'm asking you Lord to hear my prayer this day so we can testify of your healing power, both in her son and husband. Show us your glory this day Oh Lord so that others may witness your healing power. Amen."

Shirl didn't hesitate to contact the other prayer warriors in the church to stand in agreement with her on Quan's behalf. She sent a group text for everyone to pray that the brain swelling would recede by morning.

I convinced Aunt Shirl to let me relieve her of the vigil she had kept for the last 16 hours. She reluctantly went home for some much needed rest, but not before reassuring Katherine that she would be back. I sent a quick text to Coach Connors, filling him in on Quan's condition and asked him if he would ask the guys on the team to pray for him.

Once we got back to the waiting room, Katherine called her husband to update him on their son's condition. I couldn't help but notice that she was staring at me as she talked on the phone. I felt like she was going to burn a hole right through me the way her eyes were glaring at me. At one point we made eye contact but I quickly looked away, pretending I was watching the TV that was mounted on the wall. After about 10 minutes, she completed the call, but she continued to stare at me.

It made me so uncomfortable that I asked her, "Is everything okay at home?"

"Not really. My husband seems to think there's a lot more to the story than what we've been told," she replied with a smirk on her face. Then she asked, "Young man, can I ask you a question?"

"Sure, what is it?" I asked not knowing what else to say. I had a feeling where this was going, but at that point I wasn't quite sure how to avoid the inevitable.

"How did my son get mixed up with drug dealers?" she asked with an accusatory tone.

"Ma'am," I said respectfully, "I don't know. Quan was my roommate and we were teammates on the basketball team. I had no idea he was involved with these people. A couple of nights ago three guys showed up at our apartment and demanded I tell them where Quan was. I told them I didn't know and evidently that wasn't what they wanted to hear. One of them pointed a gun to my head and demanded I tell them. I have never been so scared in all my life, and even though I'm only 19, I've been through some pretty hairy situations. After they realized I wasn't lying they said to tell Quan the Rarecias brothers came by. They didn't tell me what it was about, but I knew it couldn't have been good. With the gun still pointed to my head they proceeded to warn me that if I went to the police they would find me and, in their words, 'it wouldn't be pretty.'"

"Are you selling drugs with my boy?" she asked.

"No ma'am," I said emphatically. "Why would you think I was?"

"Well," she said, "you're his roommate."

"I know," I said, "but that doesn't mean I know what he does in his spare time. With all due respect Mrs. Jeffrey," I said, "Quan is my friend and I'll admit he can be a little crazy at times; but selling drugs? I'd have to say that one caught me blindsided. One of our teammates warned me a few weeks ago to steer clear of Quan because he had heard he was dealing drugs on campus. That's the first inclination I had that anything like this was going on."

"So, you knew about this and didn't say anything to him?" she asked with a hint a sarcasm in her voice.

"Well, yes," I said, "to tell you the truth I really didn't give it too much thought because deep down I didn't want to believe that it was true. As popular as Quan is on campus, people are apt to say anything about him. That doesn't necessarily mean everything is the truth."

"Hmmm, some friend you are," she said in a rather nasty tone.

I wasn't sure if this was a mother's love or vengeance, considering my lack of experience with family dynamics. Quan was the one who brought all of this drama and pain into his family, not me. I had to admit, part of me wanted to curse this woman out for blaming me for her son's downfall, but the other part of me could somewhat empathize with what she was going through.

As I was mulling over in my mind how to respond to this would-be accusation, in walks Aunt Shirl with some sandwiches from the hospital cafeteria. I was really hungry so I dismissed my thoughts of retaliation, at least momentarily.

"Have you heard any news from the doctor today?" Shirl asked Katherine.

"No Shirl," she said, "The officers just asked me some questions about Quan, that's all."

"Well Katherine," Shirl said, "I just wanted you to know that a lot of the people at my church are praying for your son. Would you care for a sandwich?"

"No thank you," Katherine said. "I really don't have much of an appetite."

"Okay hon," Shirl responded, "just make sure you eat something later. You look a little drained, understandably so. I just want you maintain your strength."

The three of us spent the rest of the day in the ICU waiting room not saying much to one another. We were just hoping and praying that things would improve. The doctors were running a myriad of tests, checking vital signs and monitoring the swelling on Quan's brain. I had lost focus of the previous conversation with Katherine and now was riveted on the pending report from the doctor, as we all were.

After what seemed like an eternity Dr. Hunter came out to tell us the news we'd been waiting to hear. The medications were working and the swelling on Quan's brain finally had started to recede.

"Praise God, thank you Jesus," Shirl shouted as she stood to her feet. "We serve a good God who is faithful to His Word." Shirl hugged Katherine and me as Dr. Hunter looked on with a smile.

"Hopefully during the course of the next few days we'll be able to slowly ween him off this medication and allow him to wake up from the induced coma," Dr. Hunter explained. "Your son is lucky to be alive," he said looking at Katherine.

"Yes he is, yes he is," shouted Katherine as she threw her hands in the air giving praise to the One who really brought him though."

Don't Spoil My Day

"Parting is such sweet sorrow..."
--William Shakespeare

I had just gotten off the phone with my Aunt Carrol Jean and she had me hotter than a firecracker. She was blaming me for getting her sister Shirl involved with my friend's messy situation. She accused me of bringing "unneeded drama" as she put it, into the family. I couldn't wait to get off the phone with her. I was so I was grateful when I saw Heaven's number on my caller I.D. That gave me an excuse to get out from under her accusations.

"Hello Ryan, this is Heaven," she said on the other end of the phone line.

I could tell by the tone in her voice that things had definitely taken a turn for the worse. I had tried to contact her repeatedly in the last few days to update her on Quan's condition, but to no avail. I wasn't sure what was going on with her, but whatever it was it wasn't good. Maybe she was trying to distance herself from all the drama. I guess this was my introduction to understanding how women think.

"Hey babe," I said in an upbeat but quiet tone, trying not to let on I knew something was wrong, while simultaneously trying not to wake Quan who was resting in his hospital bed.

"I'm glad you called. I don't know whether or not you've been receiving my texts or not the last few days, but a lot's gone on since the last time we talked."

"Yes Ryan, I got your texts," she said, "I'm sorry for what Quan's been through. It seemed a little extreme, even if he did get burned playing with fire."

I guess she was a little miffed about the whole thing considering her standards and proactive involvement on campus. I was hoping the good news I had about Quan's improvement would be enough to change her attitude.

I could tell she had a lot on her mind so I said in the most understanding way I could, "Honey, if you need to talk I'd be glad to listen."

"Well," she said, "a lot's been going on in my life this week and I'm emotionally drained. Do you remember the last time we spoke I told you I had some business to take care of?"

"Yes," I replied, "but you never told me what it was about."

"Well, there was a reason for that. After all the whining I did to my mom about the way my dad had ditched us, she felt like he at least deserved the chance to tell me his side of the story. Evidently they had been in recent contact with one another -- I can't imagine why, but that's not my call. My mom gave my dad my cell number and he called me the other day. I can't tell you the emotions that were going through my head, hearing the voice of my real, or should I say, 'biological' father for the first time. I had seen some pictures of him, but that was the extent of the connection I had with this man."

"Did he have any explanation for what he did?" I asked, hoping this was the logical way to continue this conversation.

"If you can call it that," she said sarcastically. "My father, as much as I hate to refer to him as such, said that at that particular time in his life he made a choice to run to his addiction and away from his responsibilities. He told me had become addicted to drugs and it had such a tight grip on him that all he could think about was getting high. I guess he was also thinking about having sex with my mother, but that's beside the point. Anyway, as he continued with his sob story he told me how he had turned to a life of crime to support his habit. After he had been arrested for the eighth time he was facing some serious prison time. I guess you could call it a stroke of Divine intervention when, while serving time in the county jail, for what he didn't say, a local Pastor visited and shared the Gospel with him. My dad, for lack of a better term, told me that for the first time he heard the message of hope and redemption. You know what Ryan, he even quoted a scripture to me. He said that Pastor told him that Jesus came to 'heal the broken hearted, to proclaim liberty to the captives, and recovery of sight to the blind, and to set at liberty those who are oppressed.' He told me that he was so touched by these words and the love and compassion of God that he made a profession of faith and accepted Jesus Christ as his Lord and Savior."

Heaven continued with her story, one that I hoped would have a happy ending.

"Ryan," she said, "one day when he was scheduled to appear before the judge, an absolute miracle took place. The same

Pastor who had witnessed to him about Christ spoke to the D.A., his court appointed attorney and the judge. Instead of the judge sentencing him for his crimes there was a recommendation handed down that my dad, again if you can call him that, attend a drug treatment center that was recently opened at this Pastor's church. Upon completion of the program the judge would consider the progress of the offender as an alternate for doing prison time. Well, he successfully completed the program and the judge gave him a suspended sentence, ordered him to pay restitution and placed him on a two-year probation. If you ask me Ryan, he should have been made to pay back all the child support he owed, but then again, he wasn't on trial for that."

"Okay," I said, "keep going."

"So," Heaven said, "after he told me all of this, I asked him why he decided to contact me after all this time, 19 years to be exact. He told me he just wanted to know that I forgave him and anything after that, concerning our relationship, he would accept."

"What happened after you told him that?" I asked.

"I told him as hard as it was that I was making a choice to forgive him," Heaven said, "but I needed some time to process everything he had said. My heart was there, but the rest of me needed time to catch up."

"That's awesome news Heaven," I said. "It must have felt good to talk to your dad after all of these years and get everything off your chest. Are you planning on getting together with him and meeting him?" I asked.

"Well," she said, "I thought about it until...."

There was a long pause. I was going to interject another thought when she said, "The other day I received a collect call from the County Jail. Guess who it was?"

I knew by the tone of her voice that she was being sarcastic and really didn't expect me to respond.

"My 'supposed' dad," she said angrily.

This was terrible, I thought. Here was a man who was trying to win his way back into his daughter's heart after a lifetime of abandonment, and now this crushing disappointment. For lack of anything better to say I asked, "What did he have to say?"

"I don't know," she said, "I didn't accept the call. Whatever excuse he had this time, I didn't want to hear it. I was a fool to entertain the thought that this man had changed."

I immediately interjected, "Heaven honey wait a minute, let me say something. Sure, I get it that you're angry with your father for his past mistakes. However, I think you're being a little too hard on him. Either you're going to forgive him and let go of this whole thing, or you're going to spend the rest of your life drowning in bitter water. One minute you're preaching to me about being the change and the next you're showing me how hateful you can be. You need to make up your mind whether you want him in your life or not. The rest, in time, will take care of itself. Ain't that what the Bible says?"

"Point noted Ryan," she snapped back at me, "you just don't get it, do you? I'm tired of having to compromise so others can feel good about themselves. As far as I'm concerned, all you men are alike. Right now I'm just totally fed up with all the drama."

I could feel the frustration in her voice. I had no idea how the events of the past week had affected her. I let her continue, trying to be as respectful to her as possible.

"First," she said, "it was you seeking a pardon for your drug dealing friend -- who may have also assaulted a woman on campus -- just so I wouldn't turn his sorry butt in to the authorities. Your shortsighted empathy for your friend put me in the crosshairs of good and evil. You have no idea how offended I was when you asked me to turn a blind eye to your scheme of rescuing Quan from something he was so glaringly guilty of. I tossed and turned all that night hoping that you wouldn't get yourself in trouble implicating yourself in his mess. Can't you see that this man is your nemesis, or tell me Ryan, are you too blind to see that too? Or is this what you learned to do in prison?"

Man, she was hot. I'd never seen this side of her before.

"Heaven, honey," I pleaded, Are you implying that it's my fault Quan got beat up?"

"No, Ryan," she answered, "What I am saying is that you need to think through some of the decisions you make. You need to consider the whole picture when you make choices that could negatively affect you for the rest of your life. You knew that boy was doing all sorts of crazy and illegal things and you did absolutely nothing to stop him. Don't you see Ryan, by not becoming a part of the solution, you became just as much a part of the problem as Quan was."

Boy, all I could think was she was really unloading on me. I wasn't at all prepared for the bomb she was about to drop on me. Maybe I should have kept my mouth shut about her relationship with her father.

"Listen here Ryan," Heaven said angrily, "I'm not going to keep going on here with you. The reason I called you in the first place is because I think it's best we slow this whole thing down a notch until you get your priorities in order. Even though I have feelings for you, my convictions to please the Lord are much stronger. I've made up my mind that nothing and no one is going to come between me and my relationship with God."

"What?" I said, stunned.

"Look," she continued, "I've got three years of college behind me. I've got so much on my plate right now between studying and my commitments to maintain a safe environment on campus that frankly Ryan I don't have time for all the drama you're bringing into the picture. Not to mention this whole situation with my 'supposed' dad that just came up out of the blue. It's too much!"

I just kept my mouth shut while she vented. I was so devastated that I didn't even know how to defend myself. Part of me wanted to retaliate, yet another part of me knew that what she was saying was true. I glanced over at Quan who had remained asleep through this whole conversation. I couldn't help but wonder to myself -- had I done everything I possibly could to keep this from happening to my friend? Had I made the right choices, considering what they were costing me? Just look at all the repercussions, all the hurt and the suffering....I too had gotten caught up in the crosshairs of good and evil and was taking the fall for another man's indiscretions. Welcome to the heartache that relationships can bring into your life was all I could think.

I cleared my throat, and my mind for that matter, and asked in the most humble way I could, "Heaven, honey, do you think this is fixable? I mean, do you think we could work it out?"

It was my hope that I could convince her that what we had together would sustain us through this trial. Evidently she didn't agree.

In a cold, rather straightforward tone she said, "I don't know Ryan, we'll see in time."

Then, without any warning at all, without a chance to tell my side of the story, the phone went dead. It took me a moment to process what had just happened. I'd never been rejected by a girl before and I was crushed inside. I really liked Heaven and felt like we had a decent relationship. Hopefully things would work out between us one day. It wasn't a complete rejection, after all, I tried to convince myself, she did say "in time" things might work out.

I checked Quan one more time to make sure he was still asleep and slipped out of the room and headed down to the cafeteria to grab a bite to eat. I needed a change of scenery and some time alone to think things through. I polished off a hamburger and fries and returned to Quan's room one more time before calling it a day.

When I got back to the room, Katherine was sitting in the chair over in the corner. I barely had time to say hello when there was a knock at the door.

"Come in," Katherine said.

"Good afternoon, hope we're not intruding. My name is detective Langley and this detective Hansen," he said as they entered the room.

"No detectives, you're fine," Katherine replied.

"Yes ma'am," he said with a smile. Then he looked toward Quan who had woken up because of all the commotion in his room and said to him, "Son, you're lucky to be alive."

"Yes sir, I know," Quan mumbled through his wired jaw.

"The reason we stopped by, Mr. Jeffrey was to give you an update of the investigation," detective Langley said. "There was a camera in a nearby parking lot and it gave us a pretty good angle of what happened. We were even able to get the license plate number of a black four door truck leaving the scene. It's registered to Monti D. Rarecias of Wesley Chapel Florida. He has a long criminal record that ranges from assaults to distribution of cocaine. The list goes on and on. From the looks of it you got yourself involved with the wrong crowd Mr. Jeffrey."

Detective Langley reached into a manila folder and pulled out a picture of the alleged assailant. I got a brief glance at the picture to see if I recognized this face as one of the thugs who came to the apartment the other night. I did, but I was waiting to see if Quan was going to point him out. Quan was still in quite a bit of pain but managed to sit up as he raised the head of his bed with the remote control.

After carefully looking at the pictures Quan handed them back to the detective and mumbled a definitive, "No." Just to be sure Detective Langley heard him correctly he leaned in closer so Quan could repeat what he said. "No....it's not them," Quan said a little more emphatically.

I had a gut feeling that Quan wasn't going to give up the Rarecias brothers that easily, by positively identifying the man in the photo. Shoot, these guys were so intimidating and the reason he was in this mess was because he didn't pay them on time for drugs that were fronted to him. If I learned anything at all while I was in prison, it was to mind my own business and to keep my mouth shut. On the street your word is your bond, this is the unwritten code these men live by and for that matter, are more than willing to die for.

As I was watching all of this unfold before my eyes and the distraught look on Detective Langley's face, it was obvious that he knew that Quan was covering up for these guys. So the detective took the picture out of Quan's hand and proceeded to show it to me.

"Do you recognize this man Mr. Blake?" he asked me.

Although he looked like one of the men that was at the apartment, I could honestly say that I wasn't 100 per cent sure. I was too busy worrying about "the boss" as he called himself and the gun that was pointed at my head, wondering if he would get an itchy trigger finger and blow my brains out. I distinctly remembered a scar on the left side of his face and that wasn't evident in the picture I was looking at.

"Detective Langley," I said respectfully, "I'm just not sure. I saw the other two men briefly, but the one that held me at gunpoint, I will never forget his face. So to answer your question, I can't 100 per cent identify this man."

As I handed the picture back to the detective he said to both Quan and me, "I've got a gut feeling that you're both covering up for these guys. If I had it my way I'd haul the both of you down to the police station for lying to a law enforcement officer. You young people live by this street code that gets a lot of people killed, not to mention how hard you make it for us to solve crimes. You can't keep calling evil good, and good evil. I'm telling you, eventually it's going to catch up with you, and from the looks of it Mr. Jeffrey, it already has. I can't charge you for dealing drugs because there's no evidence to convict you, just hearsay. It would never hold up in court. This whole thing could have turned out a lot worse, so chalk it up as one of life's lessons and learn from it. And as for the both of you, stay in school and keep your nose clean. Second chances in this life are hard to come by."

He then shifted his attention directly toward Quan and said, "Mr. Jeffrey, as for the Rarecias brothers, we will be questioning the owner of the truck and keeping our eyes open for any suspicious drug activity on campus."

Detective Langley handed Quan his card and said, "If you remember anything, please give us a call."

"Thank you detectives," Katherine said. "I sure hope you catch the men who did this to my son. Please call me if you hear anything. You have my number."

With that he and the other detective walked out of the room.

Days later, when Quan was discharged, Katherine thought it would be best for him and the family if he moved back home to complete his recovery. The goodbyes at the airport were sweet. Quan hugged Shirl and promised that he would do everything in his power to pay back the money he owed her. She told him to take his time and to focus on his recovery and to get back to school, reminding him of all the potential he had for greatness. And, being the mother she was, proceeded to give him a mini-lecture about how all of the evils of society had crept into his heart and nearly destroyed his life.

"Thank you Ryan for all you did for Quan," Katherine said. "I've been watching you and realize now that I misjudged you. My son was, and is, lucky to have you as his friend." Katherine gave me a gentle kiss on the cheek and a good bye hug.

Katherine and Shirl exchanged hugs while I unloaded the luggage from the car. Quan walked over to me and wrapped his arms around me and said, "Thanks for being there for me man, I really owe you. I hope things work out between you and Heaven. I think you're made for each other. Please tell Coach Connors and the team I'm sorry I let them down. You've got my number, keep in touch."

As Quan and his mother walked away I said to Shirl, "This could have turned out a lot worse than it did. I know somehow God had His hand in all of this, and I'm so grateful for that."

"Yes sir, that's right, He sure did. What the devil meant for destruction God turned it out for our good. That's my version of Pastor Taylor's sermon on what could have happened to Joseph in the Book of Genesis. If you went to church more often you would know that Ryan," Shirl said with a smile.

FRIENDS IN HIGH PLACES

"In the end we will remember not the words of our enemies, but the silence of our friends."
--Martin Luther King Jr.

The semester ended and then the summer seemed to fly by, as it always does. The crispness in the air was a reminder of the new beginnings of another school year and the end of carefree days in the sun. I was approaching my sophomore year and was a little more comfortable with the whole school regime. I still didn't have a declared major, but I was leaning toward criminal justice. I guess it was in my blood. With all the drama that happened last year I was able to finish the school year with a 2.6 average; barely over what Coach Connors required of his players.

In addition to my upcoming studies, I had made a commitment to Aunt Shirl to work some extra hours. A few years before she had added a catering service to her bakery, and business was booming. I didn't realize she had a culinary degree from Johnson and Wales until I happened to notice it hanging on her office wall. You know, I'm glad she was prospering, she deserved it. Shirl was an intelligent, hard-working woman who has paid her dues, sacrificing and working overtime building her reputation and clientele.

I really needed the extra money, so I didn't mind spending a few hours a week and Saturday doing everything from mixing batter to filling orders to waiting on tables to running the register and even washing floors. Actually, I was grateful for the experience. I had come to realize that hard work built character, and who didn't need more of that. If all else failed I could open my own restaurant.

I thought Aunt Shirl was doing me a huge favor by working me those extra hours. Besides the money, my job was the distraction I very much needed since things didn't work out the way I planned with Heaven. Shirl seemed to sense that I was a little hurt over the whole thing. Some people call it a woman's intuition, discernment or just plain common sense. She wasn't the type to impose on a person's private space and I admired her respect for my privacy.

Even though it was a short-lived romance, I hoped that one day, after all the smoke cleared, we could be reconciled to one another. I truly regretted that my shortsightedness caused her so much stress. I had no idea how my behavior was affecting her. Call it whatever you want -- selfishness, immaturity or a breakdown in communication...I hoped the lessons I'd learned from the mistakes I made with Quan and Heaven would one day allow me to have better relationships. Outside of family, these had been the two most important people in my life, and in hindsight, I could now see how we all misunderstood each other by acting in our own best interests. This whole thing had taught me how important it is in relationships to really listen to people and try to understand their perspective. Even though Quan was being deceptive, his motives were somewhat pure, at least in his own eyes. I just wished he would have confided in me. I was still processing all the drama I had been through in the past few months and honestly work had become a welcome diversion.

As I mulled over my past, I also had to consider the blessings of the present and challenges of the future. I was so fortunate to have been given the privilege of being allowed to be a member of this family. But, as with any family, the relationships came with their unique challenges. Aunt Carrol Gene absolutely detested Shirl for "harboring a fugitive," as she put it. What my Aunt Carrol considered a curse, my Aunt Shirl saw as a blessing. I never would have dreamed that I would have been the cause of such animosity in my own family. This may be a way of life for me. Maybe it just comes with the territory for ex-cons.

Shirl, being the entrepreneur she was, catered a variety of special events in the community. The one that she enjoyed doing the most was the "Mayor's Annual Luncheon." You see, she was close friends with the Mayor's wife, Molly. I happened to be working that Saturday and it was quite the occasion. Shirl really showed out with her menu of heavy hors d'oeuvres, petite sandwiches, and a variety of fancy pastries that would rival any master baker in the state. The table was picture perfect. The lettuce avocado rolls were beautifully arranged and every dessert was baked, trimmed and strategically placed to meet Shirl's specifications.

I was totally clueless as to what it took to run a small business. There were so many factors to take into consideration -- ordering supplies, making work schedules, sanitation stipulations, customer service...the list could go on and on. I admired Shirl for her organizational and administrative skills. She took something she was passionate about, baking, and built it into a successful, thriving small business, which in turn was a wonderful asset to her family and community. Her talent and savvy business sense also came with an extra perk. Because she was in demand to cater these "high society" events, she was able to rub shoulders with some of the community's influential business and political leaders. The guest list for this event ranged from doctors to lawyers and I'm pretty sure there were a couple of Indian chiefs there too -- okay only kidding about the Indian chiefs.

We were all decked out for this occasion -- black pants, matching vests and pin-striped ties. Our dress and personal presentation complemented the beautifully decorated and arranged tables. There were vases of fresh flowers, a fountain with punch flowing from it, and if all of that wasn't enough, there was also a jazz band playing tunes under the gazebo.

"This is a pretty big deal for you," I said to Aunt Shirl.

"Yeah, it is," she replied. "Molly and I have remained friends through thick and thin. We've managed to stay close through some of the bleakest and darkest time this city has seen. From the racial riots of the 'Wilmington Ten' where nine black men and one white woman were wrongfully convicted of arson, to the hurricanes which devastated the coastline and crippled the city's infrastructure. Through it all we managed to stay in touch and remain dear friends, even after she married Mayor Kirsh. So you see Ryan, our paths often cross because she doesn't think twice about calling me to cater these types of events. It pays to have friends in high places," she said with a wink.

"That's kind of cool," I said with a smile.

The luncheon was hosted on the beachfront property the Mayor owned. The house was a huge wood frame with a sprawling backyard and an adjacent pool. I thought Shirl's house was nice. This place made Shirl's look like a shack. The kitchen looked like a dining room and the dining room looked like a ballroom.

I was browsing around admiring all of the beauty when this petite older lady bounced her way through the double doors and said with the twangiest southern drawl I'd yet to hear come out of a Carolinian, "Hey momma Shirl, come over here and give your friend a hug."

The two of them embraced with the warmest of hugs.

"It's good to see you hon," Molly said with a broad smile. "You're still looking as young as ever."

"You too Molly," Shirl chuckled.

Just then the band piped up with their rendition of "Boogie Woogie Bugle Boy" and it was on. Molly started swaying her hips to the beat of the music and simultaneously grabbed Shirl by the hand.

"Can't wait to get MY boogie on," Molly said with a grin.

"Girl, you're crazy," Shirl exclaimed. "If you keep moving like that your husband won't be able to keep up with you."

"Are you kidding!" Molly said with a loud laugh as she side stepped left to right. "He can't keep up with me when I'm not moving like this. Let me put the brakes on before my guests think I plum lost my mind."

Molly looked in my direction.

"Terrance and Tonia I've already met," she said, "but who is this strapping young man?"

"Oh forgive me," Shirl said. "This is my nephew Ryan. He's nearing the end of his summer break from college. He's a rising sophomore at UNCW."

"Ryan," Shirl said. "This is my good friend Molly Kirsh."

I greeted her with a gentle handshake and a smile and said, "Nice to meet you Mrs. Kirsh."

"Fine looking young man," Molly said with a smile as she looked Shirl's way.

"You have a lovely home ma'am," I said.

"Thank you young man," she said.

"Hey Molly, will your husband be joining us?" Shirl asked

"No honey, he's playing golf with the boys this weekend down in Georgia."

"Okay," Shirl said. "Let him know I said hello and I sent my love."

By 8:00 pm the house was abuzz with guests. Shirl had me running back and forth keeping the buffet table stocked with hor d'oeuvres and desserts. The guests were enjoying each other's company and the exotic foods and tasty desserts. There were even a few who ventured out on the lawn and danced to the tunes the jazz band was piping out.

While I was busy replenishing the appetizers I happened to see Kimberly, the co-ed I had met about a year ago at a party, out of the corner of my eye. I was surprised, to say the least, to see her at a party hosted by the Mayor's wife.

"Hey Kimberly," I said as I was placing the last tray on the table. "What in the world are you doing here?"

"Hello Ryan," she said with a warm smile. "Molly's my grandmother and I'm spending the weekend with her while Pops, I mean Grandad, is away on his golf trip."

"Well," I said. "I really thought I would never see you again after that crazy night at the party. You remember...the Courtney and Quan incident."

"Yeah," Kimberly said, looking down at her shoes. "That was a crazy night. Did your roommate ever fess up and tell you what happened that night?"

I just shook my head and said, "No. There's a lot going on with him and anyway he wound up moving back to New York to be close to his family."

Kimberly gave me a long look as though she was seriously contemplating her next remark. I really didn't want to go into any more details about Quan and was doing my best to avoid any questions. I was hoping that she would realize my awkward hesitation was a ploy to change the subject.

Just as I was going to ask about whether she was dating anyone or not she asked, "Are you still with Heaven?"

Wow, that through me for a loop.

"How did you know I was seeing her some?" I asked with a look of surprise on my face.

"Girls talk about all the hotties on campus and plus I've seen you out with her several times in the past," she said.

"No," I said. "We're not anything anymore."

I really didn't have an explanation for her and was hoping she wouldn't ask why.

To my surprise she said, "Well her loss and someone else's gain. So tell me Ryan," she asked, "what brings you to this shindig?"

"You see that lady over by the door?" I asked. "Well, she's my aunt."

"You're kidding," she said, "Shirl's your aunt? Everybody knows her. She's practically famous around here. The Cookie Shack is the best bakery in town. She's been hosting parties for my parents and grandparents for years and in fact, she baked my first birthday cake."

"Small world," I said. "I've been working at her shop off and on for the past year or so trying to make a little extra money."

Molly was still standing there, smiling. But I could only think about Heaven. "I need to get back to work here," I said. "But it's nice to talk to you again. See you back at school?"

"Sure," said Kim, smiling but looking a little disappointed. She walked away.

The night was going well. The guests were enjoying themselves and the food was a hit. I could hardly keep the tables stocked with trays. While I was carrying a tray of food from the kitchen I happened to notice something that looked out of place from out of the corner of my eye. Aunt Shirl was over in the corner talking to a man but I could see who. She seemed to be upset about something -- I could tell by the way her hands were flailing back and forth. I couldn't make out his face because his back was to me but he was a large man with broad shoulders, just like my dad. Whoever this man was, it certainly got my interest because it's very uncharacteristic for Shirl to show her emotions in public, let alone at an event where she's catering the food. Whoever he was she was definitely engaged in a heated conversation with him.

I was tempted to walk over to where they were so I could eavesdrop on what they were saying, but something told me I needed to stay put and mind my own business, which at this moment was to re-fill a shrimp platter.

MY SECRET FEAR

"Nothing in life is to be feared. It is only to be understood. Now is the time to understand more, so that we may fear less."
-- Marie Curie

The Mayor's Annual Luncheon was a hit. Molly was pleased with the way the event turned out and was very appreciative to all who contributed to its success. Shirl was even able to get a few more catering jobs, compliments of the guests who were so impressed with her cooking skills and attention to detail. I know everyone was more than impressed with Shirl's signature appetizers and classic desserts.

We had gotten home so late the previous night that I decided to skip church that morning and sleep in, in spite of Shirl's persistent knocks at my door. I just rolled over and pulled the covers over my head and pretended that I didn't hear her. "Don't get it twisted," as my momma used to say. I thought I loved the Lord as much as anyone else, but I also knew that I needed my rest. I guess I wasn't cut out for the party life.

When I finally woke up that afternoon and rolled over to look at the clock it was 2:30pm. I couldn't believe that I had slept that long. Once I had showered, I made my way down to the kitchen and made a beeline to the fridge. I proceeded to woof down some of the mini turkey burgers that were left over from the day before. Since Shirl had yet to return from church, hopefully I could cop a plea if she figured out some of them were missing.

I looked at the newest picture on the fridge and couldn't help but smile at Jaeden Henry's picture, Terrance's son. I had aspirations that this little one would be the hope this family would embrace. Sometimes it happens that way. What initially looked like such a tragedy winds up being a blessing in disguise. I remember the days when my picture graced that spot. Oh well, I thought, that's the past. There's a whole new generation on the scene now.

Shirl walked through the kitchen door before I could finish my afternoon breakfast. I noticed she had a kind of distraught look on her face and she barely managed to get out a "Hey Ryan," before she dropped her purse and Bible down on the kitchen table and headed towards the bathroom. I wasn't accustomed to this type of greeting from her. Usually she kissed my forehead and gave me a smile while she rubbed her hand gently over my head, always showing me some form of affection. Maybe she was in a hurry to get to the bathroom or she had something on her mind. Either way, this was totally out of character for her. Something was wrong. Come to think of it she just didn't seem like herself after that encounter with the mystery man the day before. They were obviously engaged in a moment of "intense fellowship" and whoever he was he certainly had quite an impact on her. I never did get a look at his face and was tempted to ask who he was, but I had a gut feeling that it wasn't the right time.

Shirl came out of the bathroom and grabbed a drink from the fridge before sitting down at the table. When our eyes met I asked her if everything was okay.

"Why are you asking?" she asked irritably.

I paused for a moment, realizing that I had struck a nerve. Then I said to her, "Aunt Shirl, yesterday at the luncheon I noticed you were arguing with a man. I was going to go over to you and make sure you were alright, but before I could you walked outside with him."

She took a long sip from her drink, methodically placed it back on the table, looked me in the eye, took a deep sigh and said, "Ryan, there's something I need to tell you and there's no easy way to say it. Did your dad ever tell you how many children Grandma and Papa Blake had?"

"Well not exactly," I said, "I just assumed it was you, him and Carrol Gene. Why do you ask?"

"Well son," Shirl said, "Momma and Daddy had a fourth son, a boy named Carlos. He is your daddy's identical twin brother."

"What? Are you kidding me? This has got to be the most screwed up thing I've ever heard...you mean to tell me my dad has a blame freakin' twin brother named Carlos?"

My father had an identical twin. If that wasn't enough to spoil my day, nothing was.

"Ryan, let me explain," Shirl continued. "All through John's and Carlos' childhood and even into adulthood they were inseparable until Carlos came home for Christmas one year and dropped a bomb on us. He told Momma he had a big announcement for us, so we automatically assumed that he had popped the question to his girlfriend at the time, Estere. When he arrived he had a big surprise, and whoa did he ever. Instead of meeting his fiancé at the front door, there stood this man named Danny with Carlos. Once again, we made the wrong assumption, thinking this was one of his friends from college. Momma, wanting to be the endearing hostess, invited them in, introduced herself to Carlos' guest and promptly asked about Estere. He said she wouldn't be joining us for Christmas this year, without any explanation as to why."

"So tell me Aunt Shirl, was the man you were arguing at the party Carlos, my dad's twin?"

"Yes it was Ryan," Shirl said.

I thought I had heard everything, but I hadn't. Shirl continued with the rest of the details.

"Let me finish the story about what happened on that Christmas Day 25 years ago. I can remember it clear as a bell. Carlos shuffled his feet and looked at the floor, trying to dodge the question before blurting out the announcement that sent shock waves through our family...and still does to this day. He told us how he had been struggling with his sexual identity. Knowing that his attractions were perverted he fell into depression and self-medicated his pain with prescription pills and alcohol. He said that his relationship with Estere was falling apart and that his grades were slipping. That's when he met Danny, our surprise Christmas guest. He said that Danny understood him and without really wanting anything to happen, they started having feelings for one another. He never did say that they were sexually active or not, but evidently that's what your dad thought. If you ask me they were. Well anyway, before Carlos could get another word out, your father went and got daddy's gun and threatened to shoot his brother and his lover if they didn't leave immediately. Well... Merry Christmas was all I could think! What a slap in the face. Ever since that day there was a bitter feud between your dad and Carlos, onethat escalated to the point of your dad denouncing his own twin as his brother. As far as John Blake was concerned, from that moment his brother Carlos never even existed."

I kept staring at Shirl with a look of shock and disbelief while I tried to process what she was telling me. Why now, of all times, was this man back on the scene and obviously causing problems again? My presence seemed to make other family members angry, so why wouldn't this estranged homosexual whose choices also threatened to destroy the stability and integrity of this family.

Before I could gather my thoughts and ask more questions, Shirl answered them.

"After you were convicted of murdering your dad, did your time and was released, Carlos found out through Carrol Jean that you were coming to live with me. Boy, I would have loved to have been a fly on the wall when that conversation went down.

Anyway, not too long after you came to stay with us I got a phone call from Carlos asking if he could meet with you. I had to say no because of the vow I made to your father years ago. In the event anything ever happened to him and I would be your guardian – and I would not allow any contact between you and Carlos. Well, I realize that you are no longer a minor, but I was still trying to protect you from all the drama."

For the first time, I was angry at Aunt Shirl. I wasn't even really sure why before I started yelling...and then it all came tumbling out.

"Protect me?" I shouted, "Give me a break. How in the hell did you do that? For the first four years and eleven months I was in prison, I never heard a word from you. You never protected me from all the hillbilly trash talkers and degenerate misfits I had to deal with, not to mention the predators. You have no idea what I went through. Yah, maybe you think I deserved it, but for you to say you promised my dad you'd be my legal guardian is a little hard for me to believe. Where were you on my birthdays and holidays? Not only did you never make an effort to come to see me, there wasn't even one card from you to let me know you cared. No hope whatsoever from you, telling me you loved me and to hang in there. I had to learn to fend for myself and fight off all the negative emotions of fear and betrayal. I'd appreciate an answer for these questions. As a matter of fact I've been wondering about it since you and Terrance picked me up when I was released. Should I call for a family meeting before you answer? Should we throw in good ole' Uncle Carlos – or do I need protection from him?"

"Listen here Ryan, don't you ever talk to me like that again, especially in my own home. I don't take that from my own children, and I certainly won't take it from you. Do you understand me? The only answer I have for you is that I needed time -- time to heal. The loss of my brother was devastating to me and it took me that long to really forgive you. I had to come to terms with that in my own soul to the point that I was ready to embrace you as a son of sorts and welcome you back into our family."

I was quiet. Aunt Shirl was quiet. I tapped my fingers on the table and finally spoke again. "Wait a minute, you need to back up little," I said raising my voice slightly. "I get the story about the bad blood between my dad and his brother, but I'm a grown man and am mature enough to come to my own conclusions. You should have told me all of this when I moved in. And what in the world was he doing at the Mayor's luncheon yesterday and why was he so angry?"

"Okay Ryan, I'm getting to that part," she said apologetically. "I just assumed that Carlos got wind that I was catering the event and showed up, rather inconspicuously, so that he could meet you. Well I was wrong. He told me that Molly had invited him and that he had no idea we would be there. It was a total coincidence that we were all there together. At my request he left, but only under the condition that I tell you about him.

And, he didn't tell me to say this, but do you remember the mystery gift of $5,000 cash and the short note that came with it?"

"You mean at the family reunion last year?" I asked.

"Yes," Shirl responded. "Also, do you recall the time you walked into my office and I pretended to be doing the books for that day and there was a bundle of cash on my desk?

"Yes Aunt Shirl," I said. "I also remember there was a manila envelope on your desk with my name and address on it. You're not telling me...."

"Yes son," she interrupted, "your Uncle Carlos was the one who gave you those gifts, hoping to bless you and win his way into your heart. I deposited the money into your trust fund. I didn't figure you'd notice or ask."

I hadn't.

Shirl, noticing the expression on my face, realized I had reached my limit with all the family secrets, the denial and whole money thing. As she reached across the table to grab my hand, I quickly pulled it away and stood up in a rage of anger and defiance so strong it surprised even me.

"You've been lying to me this whole time," I said as I pointed my finger at her. "Let me get this straight, the man I murdered for beating the crap out of me has an identical twin brother who's gay, no less, and wants to meet me. And, he's the one who gave me all that money?"

This was just too much for me to process. I didn't know whether to be angry or thankful, but the anger seemed to be winning out at that point, so without any restraint I lit into Aunt Shirl again.

"Listen to me and try to see things from my perspective if you can. For the past six years I've tried my best to erase the memory of my dad from my heart and now you tell me there's a clone of him walking around in someone else's body who has all of a sudden risen from the grave of your past. This is too much for me Aunt Shirl," I said as I headed for the door. "I've got to get out of here and clear my head."

"Ryan, honey, please don't leave," Shirl pleaded with tears rolling down her face, "we can work this out."

I just kept trucking. I felt so betrayed and was so full of anger, it really wasn't the time to talk about anything. I thought I had forgiven my father, at least I had told myself that I had. Had all those counseling sessions with Dr. Grimes been for nothing, I thought? Maybe I had just buried all that resentment and pain and had really never come to terms with it and this whole "Uncle Carlos thing" was bringing my real feelings to light. At this point I didn't even know and wasn't even sure if I wanted to. I just got into my car and sped away as fast as I could.

After I drove around aimlessly for about an hour or so, I wound up pulling into a shopping center parking lot on Market Street at around 5:00 pm. I began scrolling through my phone looking at old pictures I had downloaded from my computer....just reminiscing and trying to connect with someone from my past. I came across an old picture of my momma and me at my eighth birthday party. I remember when that picture was taken and what a happy occasion it was. I didn't have many happy memories as a boy, but I was grateful for the ones I did have.

"I miss you so much Momma," I said as I ran my hand gently across the screen. "I don't understand why things had to turn out the way they have."

I really felt like I had reached rock bottom. I hadn't felt this alone and hopeless since the first time I heard the deadbolt lock on those prison doors. All of the trauma from my past was closing in on me, not to mention the drama about Uncle Carlos. I really needed someone to talk to. I wished I could call Dr. Grimes. She always understood me and seemed to have sound advice about how to handle situations like this. But we hadn't talked much, and I didn't want to disappoint her.

As I continued to scroll through my phone, I happened to find Pastor Taylor's number. I thought about whether he would want to talk to me or not, seeing that I hadn't been that faithful in my church attendance this past year. The last time I talked to him though he really did seem to care about me. I really wanted to talk to a man and didn't have any other options at this point so I pressed his phone number and hoped for the best.

In the Likeness of my Father

"Children have never been very good at listening to their elders, but they have never failed to imitate them."
-- *James Baldwin*

"Hello," I heard on the other end of the line, "this is Pastor Taylor."

"Hey Pastor," I said, "this is Ryan, Shirl's nephew."

"Yes son, I know who you are, your name came up on my Caller ID," he said. "Is everything okay?"

"Well, not really," I said, "There's a lot going on right now and I really could use someone to talk to."

"Okay," he said, "do you need me to come to you, or would you rather come to the house?"

"I'd rather come over there Pastor," I said.

"That's just fine Ryan. You can come right over, no problem at all. When we hang up I'll text you my address, ok?" he asked.

"Ok thanks Pastor, I really appreciate it," I said.

I was only about 15 minutes from his house. He lived in a nice neighborhood near the church. I had no trouble finding the house.

I was a little nervous as I approached the front door. I knew that technically this man was my Pastor, but it had been a while since I had been in church. And besides that, we hadn't really discussed any personal issues since the last time I was in Church, about a year ago. Even though Shirl had been sending me the sermon notes on my phone, I was still coming up short with the whole "church thing." I knew Pastor Taylor was a man of God and the last time we talked he was really passionate about the Bible, but I wondered if he would understand where I was coming from. I wondered if he really cared enough to tell me the truth and to show me the love of a father that I so desperately needed.

Before I had a chance to ring the bell, I could hear the door being unlocked. They must have been watching for me from the window, I thought. Pastor Taylor opened the door and with a big smile said, "Come on in Ryan."

"Thank you Pastor," I said as I entered the foyer.

"Listen Ryan, before we go any further I want you to call me Taylor," he said as he led me into the living room."

"Beth, you remember Ryan, Shirl's nephew, don't you?" he asked his wife.

"Yes Lord," she said wrapping her arms around me in a bear hug. "Can I get you something to drink? Or maybe a sandwich or something?"

"I'm just fine ma'am," I said, "but thank you for asking."

"Okay, if I can't get you anything, I'll leave you two alone. Good to see you again, Ryan," Mrs. Taylor said.

"Ryan, let's go into my office so we can talk," Pastor Taylor said as he led me down the hallway.

When he opened the door to his office I was a little surprised by what I saw, to say the least. It wasn't at all what I expected. I thought I'd see the standard "Pastor's office" with two rusty file cabinets, remnants from a church yard sale, an old desk covered in papers and a bookcase or two filled with books about the Bible.

Instead what I saw was the ultimate "man cave," full of all kinds of sports memorabilia. There were pictures of NFL greats from the Panthers, Cowboys, Eagles and Redskins. As I panned around the room with my mouth wide open, I noticed some autographed baseball cards and hats and jerseys from various pro teams. I guess he was also a little league baseball coach, and a pretty good one at that, because above a picture of his team were some medals and trophies honoring past championships. Mixed in between all of these sports souvenirs were pictures of men Pastor Taylor must have admired; Rev. Billy Graham, Dr. Martin Luther King Jr. and Nelson Mandela. Just when I thought I had seen it all, sitting on a small desk in the corner of the room was a picture of his youngest son, Jack, that was autographed by NACAR driver Jimmy Johnson.

This was the coolest room I'd ever been in. It was a young man's dream, but there was one item that seemed strangely out of place in this "sports museum," and once I saw it I couldn't take my eyes off of it. In the center of the room on a table sat the most beautiful cross I had ever seen. It stood about two feet high and was made of chips of wood that had been glued and nailed together, intricately and painstakingly hand-sculpted to form this absolutely beautiful work of art. As I got closer to it, I noticed a small sign at the foot of the cross illuminated by a small lamp that read "Unforgettable." There had to have been a wonderful story behind the rugged design of the cross and the attached sign.

"Wow, Taylor," I said, "that's an awesome piece of artwork. I'm sure there's something more here than meets the eye. Can you tell me a little bit about it?"

"Sure Ryan," he said with a gleam in his eye. "This cross, as with any, is representative of what Christ accomplished for us at Calvary. It has a special meaning to me because the Lord gave me the inspiration for its design. You see, I used to be a missionary and my travels have taken me to every one of the 50 states. Each chip of wood represents one of the states that I ministered in and the unique people I met. There was such a reciprocity with these wonderful people. Even though my mission was to serve and bless them, they wound up blessing me in ways that I never would have known had I not gotten on their level and humbled myself as their servant."

Man this was so deep. I never realized that he had been a missionary and how much this had affected his life. I was so intrigued with the story, I forgot about my own troubles. I couldn't wait to hear the rest.

"You see son," he continued, "you don't mind if I call you son, do you? I refer to a lot of young men in that way."

"Oh no, not all," I said.

"During my travels as a missionary I met all kinds of interesting people from every walk of life, background and ethnic group. Although I was only in a relationship with them for a brief season, I came to realize that we all had something in common, our unforgettable past. Like all of us, their pasts were pock-marked with pain and suffering from the traumas caused by divorce, sickness, substance abuse and death. The root of this misery is twofold; it's consequential to living in a fallen world, something that none of us, not even the righteous, are immune to. And for others, me included, it's the fruit of the bad choices that we've made. You see Ryan, some things in this life are inevitable, while others are just symptoms of a disease called sin. God made us free moral agents for a reason. He wanted us to choose to love Him. Through what Christ accomplished for us at Calvary and acknowledging that by faith, we can now choose to have dominion over our sins. This is where we can be restored to a relationship with the One who created us, and through that communion, realize our true destiny and start bringing forth good fruit. Am I getting over your head?"

"Oh no, actually that's part of the reason I came to talk to you tonight. There's a lot going on with me, Taylor," I said holding back the tears. "There are things in my past I wouldn't want anyone to know about and just when I feel like I can keep it all managed and under control, something or someone brings all that pain to the surface, and I just can't deal with it."

"I realize that son," he said putting his hand on my shoulder. "I know all about your past, and I don't condemn you, and guess what, neither does God. Beth and I have been praying for you and it's okay if you want to pour your soul out to me now."

I really didn't know what to say, or even if I really trusted him. I wanted to, but I still had a lot of questions. How did he know about my past? I guess Aunt Shirl told him, but there's no way she could have told him everything I went through -- the pain, the confusion and the shame. Why did he care enough about me to pray for me? I wasn't even halfway faithful in church. And what about God? Where was He when I was being abused -- where was He when my mother died that horrible death, and where was He when I felt like I had no other choice than to take a life in self-defense, the life of the one who was supposed to protect me? I kept staring at the floor in silence. Pastor Taylor, realizing I was just too overwhelmed with emotion to speak, broke the awkward silence.

"Ryan, would you like me to continue with the story of the cross?" he asked pointing to the wooden sculpture.

I nodded yes.

"All of the testimonies these beautiful people shared with me were not without hope. There were the wonderful testimonies of the blessings of God, even in the midst of their suffering -- the birth of a child, seeing them graduate from college and then marry the person of their dreams. Believe me son, the testimonies of the goodness of God far outweighed the trials. And even the trials somehow God used for their benefit. He can take all of our past disappointments, even yours Ryan, and make something beautiful out of them. I know you don't read the Bible a lot, but let me reference this Scripture, Isaiah 61:2 and 3. I think it will help put what I am saying into perspective. God, in His goodness, promises us that He will, 'Comfort all those that mourn; give them beauty for ashes; the oil of joy for mourning, the garment of praise the spirit of heaviness; that they might be called trees of righteousness, the planting of the Lord, that He might be glorified.'"

Boy, that was a lot to swallow, but I was beginning to see a little bit of light at the end of the tunnel. Perhaps, somehow everything I had been through and everything I was going through now would work out.

"Is there hope for me, Taylor?" I asked.

"Well of course Ryan," he said. "None of us have gone too far, and no circumstance is too complicated, that He can't intervene and turn it around for good. Let me give you another Scripture to help you see what I'm trying to explain. In Genesis 50:20, the Bible tells us what Joseph had to say to his brothers who had persecuted him and deceived their father into thinking he was dead. I know you may not have ever heard about this story in the Bible, but it will make sense to you. It says, 'But as for you, you meant evil against me, but God meant it for good, in order to bring about as it is this day, to save many people alive.' Joseph in this story is representative of a type of Christ, someone, who although unjustly persecuted, chose to forgive and through a horrible injustice was able to bring deliverance to many. You see Ryan, Christ accomplished the same thing for us through His death, burial and resurrection. He brought hope to the lost, healing to the sick, and deliverance to the captives. It's just like this wooden cross here on this table. If you look really close you'll notice that no two pieces are alike. All the pieces are broken and disfigured in one way or another. Some are burned, while others are cracked, some as discolored, and others have the edges chipped off of them. After weeks of careful sanding, gluing and nailing I created, through the inspiration of the Holy Ghost, what I feel like is a prefect representation of the cross; a conglomeration of broken pieces of humanity who have been carefully chosen and crafted together with love to form a beautiful work of art. That work of art is the cross, the symbol of love, grace, forgiveness and redemption that was purchased with a great cost -- the sacrificial death of the sinless Son of God. One more Scripture son, if you don't mind," he said.

"No, not at all," I said, completely engrossed.

"I just can't help myself. 2 Corinthians 5:21 tells us, referring to Jesus, 'For He hath made Him to be sin for us, who knew no sin; that we might be made the righteousness of God in Him.' Amen! No matter what we've done, no matter what sins we've committed in the past, present or future, it was all absorbed in Christ, so that we would have the opportunity through repentance to be reconciled back to God. Praise the Lord!"

"Taylor, I think I get it, but I need some time to process what you're saying. There's just so much going on with me right now, so many unanswered questions," I said.

"I've planted some seeds of hope into your soul. Eventually someone else, maybe even me, will water them, but God will be the one Who will give the increase. Oops, there I go with another Bible Scripture, Anyway, I know you came over here to talk to me, and so far I'm the one that's been doing all the talking. Pastors have a tendency to do that," he said with a smile.

I was beginning to feel a little more comfortable with him now and felt like I could trust his judgment and open up to him about what happened earlier today with Shirl and Uncle Carlos.

"Well, I have a lot of trust issues because of things that have happened in my past. Today, there was a real bomb dropped on me that I had no idea how to process, so I reacted in the only way I knew how. I got angry. Aunt Shirl deceived me by never telling me my dad had an identical twin, who by the way, is gay. Uncle Carlos wanted to make his way back into my life and for whatever reason my Aunt Carrol Jean and Aunt Shirl thought it would be in my best interest if I just didn't know about him. I know they were trying to protect me, but what in the world were they thinking? Not that this is easy news to hear, but how long did they expect to keep this from me? This is so complicated. My Aunt Shirl made a vow to my dad that she would prohibit any contact by me with their brother Carlos. Talk about bad blood. Because Carlos is gay my dad threatened to kill him and renounced him as his brother, so I guess he thought that would be best for me too. And to top it all off Carlos was sending me huge sums of money anonymously to try to help me get established. I should be grateful, and I am, but I just don't know what to make of it all. Well, to make a long story short, Aunt Shirl told me all the gory details this afternoon of how she had been keeping this from me. I felt so betrayed and victimized at the same time. I really don't know what my reaction will be if I come face to face with a man who looks exactly like my dad. I'm trying to put that horrible chapter in my life behind me....and now this?" I paced back and forth nervously.

"Ryan, I can't say I know how you feel, because I've never experienced anything like you're going through. And even though Jesus never killed a man, he did experience rejection, betrayal and deceit at the hands of those whom He trusted the most. He told us in the Book of Hebrews, that He is touched with the feelings of our infirmities. See there, I only half quoted a Scripture," he said, adding an encouraging smile.

"The counsel I would give you, son, is to release your Aunts from this debt you feel like they owe you. I'm sure they meant well and were only acting out of love for you. They wanted to protect you, they just made assumptions on your behalf and did the right thing the wrong way. As far as your Uncle Carlos, even though he may resemble your father in many ways, he's not your father. He's a man, with obvious faults, who, after you get to know him, may not be anything like your dad. Give him the grace to be who he is and be willing to meet him where he is. Let God work out the rest, and if you trust Him, believe me, He will," he said putting his arm around my shoulder.

I thought about how no one had "protected" me in prison – and thought about telling him how Aunt Shirl hadn't talked to me while I was there, but I sensed I didn't need to.

I didn't have a response for what the Pastor just said, but something deep in my soul knew that he was right. The way he looked at me, I even wondered if he hadn't privately helped Aunt Shirl forgive me and take me in. Yes, I was still angry, still hurt, but what he said gave me some hope. I guess it was time I stopped thinking about my own pain and started realizing what other people are going through too.

"Okay Taylor, thanks. I'll think about what you said, I just need some time to sort out all my feelings," I said.

"I know Ryan, I know. Let me give you a little insight into the heart of God. We all, you, me, Uncle Carlos, exist because of God. We're not a biological accident, no matter what you've been told. God is the One who ordains life and we are all fearfully and wonderfully made, created in His image and likeness and for His glory. We all have our own destinies to fulfill and are uniquely designed by Him to fulfill those destinies. Even before you were born, Ryan, God knew what you would look like, even your personality and the talents and abilities that He would give you the stewardship over. This beautiful story is encapsulated in the first two chapters of the book of Genesis. God spoke His whole creation into existence in six days. On the seventh day He rested, not because He was tired, but because He had someone, Man, to rest and fellowship with. Are you still following along with me okay?" he asked.

"Yes, absolutely," I said.

"Ok good," he replied. "As you've probably noticed, sometimes I get on a roll and I don't realize I'm losing people. After God created man He placed him a beautiful garden called Eden, to dress and to keep it. At this point in creation there were no weeds, thorns or thistles. All Adam had to do was manage the garden and exercise dominion over God's creation. Quite the ideal situation, wouldn't you say?" he asked.

"Yes," I said, "it doesn't look like anything could have gone wrong."

"Well," Pastor Taylor said, "a couple of things went wrong. First of all, there was one stipulation God required of man. Remember, when we're in a covenant with God, the agreement is based on His conditions, not ours. Nor is it based on our interpretation of those conditions. He gave Adam the liberty to make any choice he wanted while governing and overseeing the creation -- just refrain from eating from the tree of the knowledge of good and evil. Doesn't sound too difficult, does it? Well, let's see what happened next. God had complemented Himself on the completed work of His creation by saying to Himself and the Godhead, 'it is very good.' But when it came to Adam being alone God said, 'it is not good.' Mind you, Adam was alone with God and God Himself said that this was not good. I tell that to people who think they can have their own little personal relationship with Him outside of the fellowship of the church.

Anyway, along comes woman on the scene. This is the one the serpent tempted concerning eating the fruit of the forbidden tree. Adam also partook of the tree, but his motives were different than the woman's. She was enticed through the un-surrendered appetites of her soul, namely the lust of her eyes, the lust of her flesh and the pride of life. Believe me, all of this is in the Bible. It's in Genesis Chapter 3 and 1 John 2:16. Adam was not deceived, but sinned with his eyes wide open. Some theologians say that he was acting as a type of Christ, dying for his bride. Well, the jury's still out on that one, but the point is, Ryan, the woman was beguiled, and Adam, regardless of his motives, suffered the same consequences as her. This is what is referred to as the fall. God, in His omniscience knew this would happen, but in his love for Adam and Eve and all of mankind made reconciliation possible by determining another's destiny, His only begotten son's. The Bible tells us that Jesus was the Lamb slain before the foundation of the world. Still with me?" he asked.

"Yup, I think so. I've never heard it explained to me like that. I had some idea what happened, but never knew why. I always thought God was mad at us."

"No Ryan, not at all. He loves us and wants nothing more than to have a relationship with us, like it was in the Garden before the fall when His voice walked with Adam and Eve in the cool of the day," he said. "What I've been trying to do is lay the groundwork for some pretty heavy theological teachings in the most basic way I know how. I want you to understand why you are here, God's plan for your life, and how to have a meaningful relationship with Him and others, especially people you don't understand. I don't really know how to make it any more plain to you than this. God loves you and has a great plan for your life, providing you submit to His will. He has given you the dominion over His creation, but you must be willing to govern on the terms outlined in His covenant, the Bible. You have tremendous potential because of the Divine attributes intrinsic to your being, but those can only be realized through a relationship with Him."

I was listening as intently as I could, but as I glanced out the window I couldn't help but notice the two birds perched on a tree limb nestled together as though they didn't have a care in the world. I wished my life was that simple.

"Ryan," Pastor Taylor said interrupting my thoughts, "I don't have an explanation for everything that happened to you, but you have to believe that somehow God will take that mess and work it out for your good. And He will if you love Him and answer His call. That's my last Scripture for the night, I promise."

Since I wasn't quite sure at this point what my purpose was in life, I realized through this conversation with Pastor Taylor that everything, the way I interpreted my past, engaged my present and aspired for my future, hinged on my relationship with God.

Until I got to the place that I fully embraced these teachings, he encouraged me to experiment with different areas of service. He told me that as far as he could tell, I was a good student in college, a hard worker and, more than anything, willing to listen and learn from people who loved me and had wisdom.

He told me how much I had to be grateful for and even offered to be my mentor. This was something I'd always longed for, a man who really cared about my well-being, speaking truth into my life while showing me what it looked like to be a man, a real man that is. He gave me so much hope, so much to look forward to, and yes, so much I needed to work on.

It was so late when Pastor Taylor and I finished talking that I wound up spending the night. I said my goodbyes, promising that I would attend church the following Sunday. When I got home I expected to find Shirl sitting at the kitchen table drinking her morning coffee. Since she wasn't there I went upstairs and knocked on her door.

"Come in," she said.

Shirl was sitting in her rocking chair sifting through some old photo albums. Tonia had tried to get her to put them into a digital format, but Shirl replied, "The old way still works best for me."

"Hey Ryan come on in," she said.

"Good morning Aunt Shirl, what cha up to? I asked as I sat on the bed next to her. She looked up at me, poised to answer, but I cut her off before she respond. "Before you say anything Shirl, I want to apologize for lashing out at you yesterday. When you dropped that bombshell on me I immediately ran for cover so I wouldn't have to face all the lies and deceptions. It was so traumatizing. Truth is, I never want to deal with anything or anyone that reminds me of my dad. What hurts me most is that you knew about this the whole time and kept it from me, hoping that your little family secret wouldn't slip out. The least you could have done was told me about Uncle Carlos so I could have better prepared myself."

"Ryan, honey, believe me I wanted to, but I just didn't want anything standing in the way of me loving you all over again."

"You know Shirl," I continued, "my dad even blamed me for my mother's death. She would have never been on the road that day if I hadn't gotten into a fight at school. I'm sure you remember all of this. I sat in the principal's office for hours waiting for her before they came and told me about the accident. When I heard the news I felt like someone had punched me in the stomach. I relived that feeling for months because my father kept blaming me for the accident. The physical and emotional abuse became a daily ritual with him. At one point he even locked me in the dog's cage all night because I didn't do my chores. He told me that this is what happens to criminals who fail to listen and who break the law. Can you imagine being locked in a dog cage? I felt humiliated in the worst kind of way."

At this point tears started rolling down my cheeks and I said, "You know, I never really meant to shoot my father, but he kept coming after me. I had no other choice and it came down to him or me. I'll never forget the look in his eyes and I honestly don't know if I'm prepared to stare into Uncle Carlos' eyes either."

"Ryan," Shirl said as she took my hand, "I would never have thought a father, much less my brother, would subject his own child to that kind of abuse. John called me the day before he was murdered and told me that he had lost his job and was worried about how he was going to support you. Your dad was a proud man and didn't like to burden other people with his problems. You know, looking back he may have been reaching out to me for help. I was so wrapped up with my family and the business that I may have missed it. I really should have been there for him after your mom passed. If I had been more involved in your lives, I might have seen some of the warning signs. I wish you would have called me and told me."

"Aunt Shirl," I said, "I knew my dad was under investigation for letting Mr. Roanoke off when he pulled him over that morning, even though he smelled alcohol on his breath. But I didn't realize that my dad would lose his job a few months later. I wonder if the fact that he was drinking heavily at the time had anything to do with it?"

Shirl said, "Quite possibly. Listen here Ryan, I was wrong for not telling you about your father's twin. I wanted everything to be perfect when you came to live with us. You'd already been through so much. Just realize your Auntie loves you like you were my own and all I want is the best for you. Mothers tend to be a little overprotective when it comes to their young'uns. So will you forgive your Auntie Shirl and give her a grace pass?"

"Yes," I said as we embraced, "you're the only family I have. As for Uncle Carlos, I' be willing to meet him, and I appreciate what he's done for me but I can't make any promises."

"I know Ryan, I know," she said.

FINALLY

"What feels like the end is often the beginning."
-- Anonymous

Summer had come and gone, too fast as always. It had been a busy day for me on campus, getting my class schedule, dorm assignment and getting hooked up with the guys on the ball team. After dinner in the dining room I returned to my dorm to lay down and take a nap.

I woke up in the middle of the night, drenched in a cold sweat from a dream I was having. In this dream, my mother and I were sitting on the porch of an old abandoned house. She was telling me how handsome I looked and how proud she was of everything I had accomplished. She asked me if I was happy with Aunt Shirl.

I replied, "Yes, momma, she's been taking good care of me."

Mom grabbed my hand and said, "Your father sends his love and he wants you to forgive him."

"Momma I already have, a long time ago," I said assuredly.

I asked her about Uncle Carlos and she said with a grin, "He's a good man, give him a chance."

Our conversation was suddenly interrupted by a loud trumpet blast.

"He's calling," she said turning to walk away from me. "I've got to go," she said as her image gradually began to fade away into the clouds.

I jumped off the porch and ran to her crying, "Don't go -- stay a little longer."

"Don't worry son, I'm always with you," I heard her say.

After I woke up I laid in the bed for a few moments hoping I would fall asleep again and be able to return to the dream, but it didn't happen. She'd been dead for about seven years and I'd never dreamt about her before. I couldn't wait till morning so I could call Aunt Shirl and tell her about the dream.

When the morning finally came, it was the first thing I did. "Aunt Shirl," I said excitedly.

"Yes Ryan, is everything okay? You sound a little excited," she said.

"I'm okay. I had the most wonderful dream last night. I dreamed that I saw my momma and she looked so beautiful and peaceful. She told me that she was proud of me and assured me that she's always with me."

"Wonderful, wonderful," she said. "Take heart to what your momma said. I miss her a lot too. Listen Ryan, I don't mean to cut you short, but I was heading out the door for work. You can fill me in next time you come home, okay sweetie?"

"Okay Aunt Shirl, have a good day," I said.

Our basketball team won their first away game. Ty hit the game winning shot in the final second. It was such a sweet victory and we needed that shot of adrenalin at the beginning of the season. The two hour bus ride on the way home was filled with jokes, rough housing and loud laughter.

By the time we got back to the campus it was about 10:00pm. A couple of my teammates invited me to hang out at the lounge. It's a place to gather together with friends, shoot the jive and celebrate our victory with food and drinks. As soon as I walked in the door I saw Heaven standing in the corner talking with some girls. She looked my way and gave me a brief smile. We hadn't spoken since that last phone call when Quan was in the hospital so I wasn't quite sure how she would respond if I walked over to talk to her. With the past 12 hours of the day going as well as they had I thought, "what have I got to lose?" So I stepped out on faith and walked over to her.

"Hey ladies, what's going on?" I asked.

"Nothing much," they responded in unison.

"Heaven, could I speak to you privately for a sec?" I asked.

"Sure Ryan," Heaven answered, "I'll be right back girls, find us a table."

We both walked outside onto the deck where it wasn't so noisy.

"What's up Ryan?" she asked.

"Nothing much, just wanted to see how you've been doing. I haven't seen you in about four months," I replied.

"I didn't realize that it had been that long. Congratulations on your win," she said.

"Thanks. How's your family doing? I mean, how did things work out with your dad?" I asked.

"A lot better than I ever would have thought. Do you remember when I told you about not accepting a collect call from him because he was in jail?" she asked.

"Yes," I replied.

"Well as it turned out a previous charge of misdemeanor breaking and entering was overlooked by the clerk. So a warrant was issued and he was arrested. After his lawyer heard about it he took care of the matter in court and my father was released. Small price to pay for past mistakes. But that's just part of the story. We actually met each other for the first time a couple of months ago and he has become very much a part of my life. You know, I even look like him. I feel more complete now than I ever have. I'm thanking the Lord for softening my heart so that I could forgive him and for making my family complete."

"Awesome news Heaven, it must feel good to have your father involved in your life."

"Yeah, it sure does. Ryan I want to apologize to you for how I acted a couple of months ago. You've always been nice to me and I was kind of unreasonable about the whole situation. All the drama with my dad and your crazy roommate really had me stressed out. It was no offense to you. I just couldn't handle it all at one time, especially when I was becoming emotionally attached to you."

"Did I hear you correctly? You actually had feelings for me?"

"Yes I did, and still do. Seeing you tonight reminded me of how much I miss your fine self."

I was speechless. I didn't think she had feelings for me at all. I know she must have thought I was a little foolish, with this huge grin on my face that stretched from ear to ear.

I embraced her with a gentle hug and whispered in her ear, "I forgive you honey." I placed a gentle kiss on her cheek. "I really missed you."

"I missed you too Ryan."

"Heaven, I owe you an apology for being so selfish. I never meant to hurt you. I was so wrapped up in the whole mess with Quan that I really didn't consider how that would affect our relationship. Nor did I consider how it would affect my response to what you were going through. Please forgive me."

She smiled and gave me a delightful wink and said, "You're good, don't let it happen again, or else."

I knew there had to be a time when I told her about my past. I wasn't sure how the fact that I killed my father would affect our relationship. I had rehearsed this speech in my mind a couple of times and figured this would be as good a time as any to tell her.

"Heaven," I said looking in her eyes, "I've got something I need to tell you before this relationship goes any further."

"Okay, go ahead," she said.

"Remember when you asked me about my family and I told you how after both my parents were killed in an accident Aunt Shirl took me in?

"Yes Ryan, I remember," she said.

"Well that was only half the truth. My mom was killed by a drunk driver when I was 13 years old. She was on the way to my school because I had gotten into some trouble. After that my father started drinking a lot and became very physically and verbally abusive to me. One night when he was really drunk he beat me so badly that I took his gun and killed him. You see Heaven, I realize now looking back how much pain he must have been in. My Aunt Shirl just recently told me that he had lost his job as a County Sherriff. His whole world had caved in and once the alcohol got in him, I was the one he took frustrations out on. I was sentenced to five years at Camp Penitude for juveniles. I've repented to the Lord for this sin and while I was incarcerated I received counseling. I blame myself for both of my parents' deaths."

I wasn't quite sure what her reaction would be. She kind of had that deer in the headlights look.

"Let me finish the story, okay?" I asked.

She just nodded.

"Aunt Shirl's been such a blessing to me. Now I have a home and a family, a part time job and I'm getting my education. But the best thing of all is I have you, don't I?"

She took me by the hand and with tears in her eyes said, "What a terrible tragedy. You've lost both of your parents. I know the Lord has forgiven you, so how can I hold this against you."

"Thank you honey, thank you so much," I said with tears rolling down my face.

"There's one more twist to this drama, that is if you can stand it?" I asked.

"It couldn't get any worse," she said with a smile.

"As it turns out my dad had an identical twin brother, who just so happens to be gay. He wants very much to be a part of my life and has even given me money to help me get back on my feet. I'm really not sure I'm quite up to meeting someone who looks exactly like my dad. Anyway, I told my Pastor and he agreed to be in prayer about it."

"Okay," she said. "I'll be in prayer with him. Your uncle probably loves you very much and wants to help you. It is a little strange though that there's a man out there who looks just like the man who caused you so much pain. I'm sorry you had to go through that, but I wouldn't be surprised the way my God works --if He doesn't bring about good for everyone involved -- you, me, Uncle Carlos and anybody else in your family. Just be patient Ryan."

"Ok Heaven," I said squeezing her hand. "Thanks for being so understanding."

Heaven and I walked back into the lounge and lo and behold across the room stood Kim talking with a group of other coeds. I was a little nervous to say the least and stood there for a moment not really knowing what to do.

"You okay Ryan?" Heaven asked. "You look like you just saw a ghost."

"Yah, I'm okay honey. You remember the night I took you to Laura's for dinner and I told you about a girl named Kim that I had met at a party?"

"Yes, I remember."

"Well she's standing right over there," I said pointing Kim's way.

"Why don't you introduce her to me?"

"Okay, come on," I said.

We walked over toward Kim and I performed the introductions, giving Kim a friendly hug.

"Nice to meet you Heaven. Great game tonight Ryan -- you really did your thing," Kim said looking my way, "I have to say, you two make a beautiful couple. If you don't mind I'm going to excuse myself and get back to talking with the girls. Enjoy the party two."

Well that was pretty painless, was all I could think.

Heaven and I spent the rest of the evening talking and catching up with one another. It's amazing how much can happen in a person's life in 4 months. It was almost midnight by the time we finished talking. I gave her a goodnight kiss and told her I would be in touch. We both got in our respective cars and drove home. I didn't want to spend that weekend at the dorm, but wanted to spend as many weekends at home so that I could spend more time in church.

Sunday morning rolled in faster than I thought it would. I didn't get up in time for church and felt kind of guilty about it. I understood most of what Pastor Taylor was telling me about God.

I knew that the Lord was the answer to all of my problems, or at least He was the One who could help me deal with them.

As I made my way downstairs, I noticed how fresh and clean the house smelled. Shirl was not only a great cook, but a great housekeeper too. Nothing was ever out of place. She had left me a sticky note on the counter which said, "Will be home after church. There's some lasagna on the bottom shelf of the fridge."

Before I was able to finish fixing my lunch the doorbell rang. I grabbed my bowl of lasagna out of the microwave and hurried to the door. I opened the door and there stood this tall slender man who resembled my father. His facial features were very similar to my dad's and his build was the same too. We stood there momentarily in a stance position eyeing each other down like two animals preparing to pounce on each other. I ran my eyes slowly up and down him looking for flaws, but could find none. It was him, the secret man everyone was withholding from me, standing just inches from my face.

This wasn't anything like I expected. The dread and fear I thought I was going to experience wasn't there. All I could see in his eyes was kindness and gentleness and a desire to be accepted.

"You must be Ryan," he said softly.

"Yes I am," I said. "You must be Uncle Carlos."

"It's nice to meet you," I said as I extended my hand to give him a firm handshake. "I've heard so much about you."

"Likewise, it's an honor to finally get to meet you nephew," he responded.

We just stood there like two statues smiling at one another. Finally he asked me if I was ever going to invite him in.

We went into the dining room. I offered him a cup of coffee before we sat together at the dining room table. We spent the next hour or so getting to know each other. I asked him a lot of questions, some about his life and some about my parents, especially my dad. I didn't want to get too personal -- after all this was our first meeting. He was surprisingly open to me about his life. I felt like he was a connection to my past, in a different way than Aunt Shirl was. Here's a man who knew my dad from the time he was born. I was so interested in seeing the side of my father that he knew. I listened to stories about things they enjoyed together growing up -- fun times, family times. I could see how having Uncle Carlos in my life would be a great benefit to me. I hoped that he felt the same way about me.

We were just starting to get to know each other when I heard the sound of keys rattling in the door.

"That's Aunt Shirl coming home from church," I said.

As she came through the door and looked towards us she said, "Well I see you two have finally met."

"Yeah Shirl," Carlos said standing to give her a hug. "I came over to see my baby sister and my niece and nephew and plus I wanted to introduce myself to my other nephew Ryan."

"We're all doing well thank you and how about yourself? Are you staying out of trouble?" Shirl asked.

"Yes momma," Carlos replied as he winked at me.

I noticed Shirl glanced my way to see what my facial expression looked like. I nodded at her to let her know that everything was alright between Uncle Carlos and me.

Uncle Carlos got up and said that he needed to be getting back home. Before he left he reached into his jacket pocket and pulled out a business card. He handed it to me and said, "Call me if you need me for anything."

"Will do, uncle," I said, surprising even myself.

Can you Withstand the Storm?

"Weeping may endure for the night, but joy comes in the morning."
-- Psalms 30:5 NKJV

With the Thanksgiving holiday just a few days away, Shirl was planning on having as many of the Blake Family clan as possible in attendance for dinner. Not only was this a big family celebration, but she told me she had her heart set on a big turnout for the Sunday service prior to the holiday extravaganza. Pastor Taylor had hinted to her that he would be starting a series of messages that would be focusing on family values, forgiveness and restoration. Shirl told me that she had sent out a text to her brother Carlos and her sister Carrol Jean inviting them to the service. She also told me that she fully expected me, Tonia and Terrance to also be there.

I hadn't exactly been faithful to church since the last time I'd spoken with Pastor Taylor. I knew I had to make a decision about serving God, I just wasn't sure I was willing to make that commitment. For the first time in my life things seemed to be working out for me. I had what I'd always longed for -- a loving family, a beautiful girlfriend, I was in college, and I had a little money. Don't ask me how I felt like a relationship with God would compromise that.

Well Sunday morning came. We were all dressed up in our best duds. I'd managed to graduate from my outlet store wardrobe of kakis and a knock off Polo shirt. Terrance took me shopping one weekend before the start of school this year and I bought some really cool clothes. But more importantly. Heaven liked my style too. I had called her the night before and invited her to come to church with us. I left a little early to go pick her up.

Heaven and I arrived just in time for the service to start. Maybe it was my imagination, but it seemed like there were a lot more people there than there were the last time I attended. Maybe the upcoming holiday had something to do with it, or it was due to the sermon series Pastor was starting this week. I don't know. All I know is there was barely enough room in the pew for Heaven and I to squeeze in next to Aunt Shirl. Terrance, Anna, baby Jaeden and Tonia sat to her left. I noticed Aunt Carrol Jean was sitting behind us and I gave her a wave and a half of a smile. Deep down I felt like she hated me. I can't help what happened in my past. Maybe Pastor's sermon would help us all. God knows we still needed it.

"Good morning congregation of Landfall United Methodist Church," Pastor Taylor said loudly.

"Good morning Pastor," we all answered in unison.

"It's good to see everyone in the house of the Lord on this fine November Lord's day. Let's turn the service over to our praise and worship leader Anita Holmes."

"Thank you Pastor," she said. "Will y'all please stand while we sing to our Lord the praises He most certainly deserves."

We all stood and sang a few songs, my favorite was "Amazing Grace." It felt so good to be with people who loved God. I guess I didn't know what I was missing not coming to church any more than I did. It was the same feeling I had when I knew I was accepted by Shirl and her family, only better. I knew that God had somehow watched over me, because if he hadn't I would have died at the hands of my own father. Really deep down I was mad at God for allowing me to go through what I did. He could have stopped it, but then would there be this wonderful family reunion that we were experiencing today? I wondered if Uncle Carlos was going to be here? I knew Shirl had invited him. Anyway I'd made up my mind I was going to enjoy this moment.

Pastor Taylor took his place behind the pulpit.

"If you have your Bibles congregation, please turn to Matthew Chapter 7 Verses 24 through 27. Don't ask me why someone would come to church without their Bible, but anyway if you don't have yours there's one under the chair in front of you. Amen."

That someone who didn't come to church with his Bible was me. I grabbed one that was conveniently located on the back of the pew in front of us and Heaven was gracious enough to help me find my place.

"When you've found Matthew 7 Verse 24 say Amen," Pastor Taylor said.

After hearing the pages turning the church (me included) responded with a loud "Amen."

"Now the word of God reads: 'Therefore whoever hears these sayings of Mine, and does them, I will liken him to the wise man who built his house on the rock: and the rain descended, the floods came, and the winds blew and beat on that house; and it did not fall, for it was founded on the rock. But everyone who hears these sayings of Mine, and does not do them, will be like a foolish man who built his house on the sand -- and the rain descended, the floods came, and winds blew and beat on that house, and it fell. And great was its fall.'"

"For the past month I've observed many families in the congregation go through some trials and tribulations. Some of you made it through those trials and some of you didn't. You gave up and threw in the towel, or worse yet blamed God for your misfortune."

Ouch, I thought. I was just thinking how I was mad at God for allowing me to suffer like I did when He could have very well done something about it. Now I knew what it meant to get your toes stepped on in church. But even more than that, were these church-going Christians also mad at God? I was beginning to wonder if there's hope for any of us. I knew I needed to hear what Pastor Taylor had to say, and evidently everyone there did too.

"Life sure has its way of knocking you upside the head; can I get a witness?" Pastor Taylor said as he pounded the pulpit.

"Amen," we all responded together.

"We pray, fast, read our Bibles and attend church every time the doors are open. Yet the Lord seems to be distant, our prayers go unanswered, or at least we think they do. We need to realize that when we don't get the answer we feel we should, at the time we think we should, in the way we think we should, that the Lord is working a lot more behind the scenes than just answering our request. That's a lot of shoulds, ain't it? That's a whole lot of us and not too much of God. I'm telling you through experience that sometimes it's timing, sometime it's a greater work than what you could ever imagine and all the pieces have yet to fall in place. So, what happens in those times of testing is that our faith gets kind of shaky and some of you develop a sense of hopelessness."

Even though I had not always considered myself to be "religious." I believed in God. So far this sermon wasn't doing me any favors. But I came for Aunt Shirl and because I truly felt like Pastor Taylor cared about me.

"In our text today we're talking about two different people -- the wise man and the foolish man. In my opinion, which is deeply influenced by the Lord, both of these men had an agenda. They both wanted a safe place, a haven, a home to raise a family, pay off a mortgage, and have an inheritance to pass down to the next generation. It's what we all want in our hearts, isn't it?"

"Amen," the congregation echoed.

"On the surface these men were probably good, hard working men, who lived in the same community, went to church and paid their tithes. You know, family men who wanted the best for their wives and children. The difference between these men is after they both heard the word of God and the design specifications for building a house, one decided to take heed and build according to God's plan and the other decided to do things his own way. And you see the results in the last two verses of our text."

I noticed Uncle Carlos out of the corner of my eye. He was walking down the aisle and took a seat next to Aunt Carrol in the pew behind us. He tapped Aunt Shirl on the shoulder to let her know he was there and looked over at me and nodded his head.

The pastor continued with his sermon.

"There are three reasons God gives us His Word. It's either to warn us, correct us or to help us prosper. Just like in the days of Noah. God gave him explicit instructions to construct an ark of gopher wood and to cover the entire structure with pitch. The design had to be to God's exact stipulations and dimensions. The length of the ark was to be 300 cubits, which incidentally is 450 feet. The width was to be fifty cubits which is 75 feet and the height was to be 30 cubits which comes out to be 45 feet. Now, stay with me people. I'm trying to show you something here. God had His reasons for being so exact in his design. He also told Noah to put a window on the top of it and a door on the side and to make it three stories high. Let's turn to that place in Scripture so I don't misquote it. Let's see...turn to Genesis Chapter 6. Let's start with verse five and read through verse eight. Everybody with me?"

Again there was a unanimous, "Amen." I was able to find this chapter in the Bible because I knew Genesis was the first book. I looked over at Heaven and gave her a wink.

Pastor Taylor read from the Bible.

"Then the LORD saw that the wickedness of man was great in the earth, and that every intent of the thoughts of his heart was only evil continually. And the LORD was sorry that He had made man on the earth, and He was grieved in His heart. So the LORD said, 'I will destroy man whom I have created from the face of the earth, both man and beast, creeping thing and birds of the air, for I am sorry that I have made them. But Noah found grace in the eyes of the LORD.' That word grace in the context of that verse means favor."

"Let's jump down to verse 22 of the same chapter. It reads 'Thus Noah did according to all that God commanded him, so he did.' So you see church, for Noah and his family were to survive he had to prepare an ark of safety for them. In 2 Peter, Chapter two, Verse five the Bible tells us 'and (God) did not spare the ancient world, but saved Noah, one of eight people, a preacher of righteousness, bringing in the flood, on the world of the ungodly.' When I, and other Pastors like me, stand in the place of God, in the stead of God, and bring forth the word of life, our goal is to help you to build a spiritual house based on sound doctrine. Because God loves us, His desire is for us to have hope and faith. God tells us that because He first loved us we can love Him. And through that love we can trust Him through faith, and that faith gives us hope."

This sermon was a whole lot more than I, or anyone else ever bargained for. But I was beginning to understand the heart of God. He had a standard that can only be met through a relationship with Him. He judges sin, but not willingly, but because He cannot condone anything that is not consistent with His character. I was beginning to wonder where I fit into the scenario of this sermon.

But Pastor Taylor still had more to say.

"Church family, it's just like our first text this morning. Both of the men who built houses, whether on the rock of Christ or the shifting sands of the world, experienced a storm. It's not if the storms come, but when. They're going to come, believe me. The rain, winds and floods are the trying of your faith through circumstances, through losses, and even through misunderstandings. Family crises, you name it. Sometimes it will start off with a few drops, like your child being disrespectful, or maybe hanging around with the wrong crowd, experimenting with drugs or skipping school. You don't think too much about it because you just assume they are going through adolescence and they're looking for attention....something that will pass with time. There is so much confusion amongst young people today because of the divorce rate and women raising children without a father in the home. You may even blame some of your struggles on heredity, poor examples, or no examples. The rain drops you have ignored all these years have started to pour heavily on your family and it's taking its toll in physical sickness and emotional stress. The family issues are coming at you from every angle and the problems are mounting up. Now the child who was just experimenting with drugs has become an addict and possibly facing prison time. Your teenaged daughter has become pregnant and you're planning a wedding before her man has time to change his mind. You work hard on your job with expectations of a promotion only to find out that you've been laid off due to budget cuts. You get behind on your mortgage, your car is repossessed and you're on the verge of bankruptcy. The rains of disappointment are flooding out your faith and causing you to doubt the very foundation of your faith... Christ. The sweet promises of His word are drowned out by the raging storms of life. While you're braving the storm, the rains and gale force winds keep coming, badgering you on every side. They throw you off balance and leave your mind wandering and in a state of confusion. The enemy of your faith, fear, takes up residence in your soul, and you start questioning the validity of God's word. Trust me, church, when you find yourself in this state you have to be careful who you listen to. Not everyone who calls themselves a Pastor or teacher has your best interest at heart."

This kept getting hotter and hotter. I was beginning to wonder if there was a way out of these predicaments. Surely there was hope for people like me. I needed to hear the rest of the story.

Pastor Taylor started winding down his sermon.

"Now I don't want to finish this sermon today without telling you that you can have all the degrees, awards and certificates from any of the prestigious colleges in the land. You can be saved, sanctified and filled with the Holy Ghost and the storms of life will still beat on your house. Like I said brothers and sisters, life in this fallen world is indiscriminate, meaning it covers both ends of the spectrum, and everyone in between.

But here's the difference -- are you going to build your life God's way or your own way? Both men went through the same storm. The consequences were the same for them both, but we see different results. One man lost all of his investment in life. The Bible tells us that his house fell, and great was the fall thereof. The storm left him physically and emotionally bankrupt. He had nothing left to rebuild with. All of his resources were depleted. In John 10:10 Jesus tells us that the 'thief comes to steal, kill and destroy.' But the rest of that verse tells us the 'I have come that you might have life, and life more abundantly.' Amen Church! The abundant life is a life worth living. We serve God for who we'll become not for how He blesses us. And He's such a wonderful Father He blesses us anyway.

So the question before my congregation this morning is can you withstand the storm? If not, I'm asking you to come to this altar and begin that process of building your house on a firm foundation."

As Ms. Holmes began playing a song, everybody stood to their feet. I knew that this message was for me, if it wasn't for anyone else in the congregation. I held Heaven's hand and I could hear her praying for me quietly. I said in my heart, "Lord I know I need to make a decision, I just want to know if I can trust you, I don't know if I can live this." It just so happened Ms. Holmes was singing "Trust and Obey." The chorus goes like this: "For there's no other way to be happy in Jesus, than to trust and obey."

If that wasn't a sign from the Lord I didn't know what else could have been. I realized I was at a crossroads in my life and I needed to make a decision. All the pain, the heartache and the sin of the past could be wiped away in one moment. The God that I was so angry with and misunderstood so much all of my life was the One who was willing to accept me as his son, just as I am.

I could now have the Father I always wanted.

With tears in my eyes I stepped into the aisle and made my way to the altar. I could hear the quiet sobs and sighs of family members and Heaven. Shirl even whispered a soft "Hallelujah, thank you Jesus."

As I made my way to the altar Pastor Taylor was standing there with tears running down his face. He said to me, "Son are you ready to surrender your life to the Lord?"

"Yes Pastor," I said.

"Alright, I want you to pray this prayer with me. 'Father, I acknowledge that I am a sinner, lost and undone and out of covenant with you. Please forgive me of all my sins. I believe you sent your only begotten Son, Jesus, as the spotless Lamb to shed his blood and die for me on Calvary's cross. I believe He rose from the dead on the third day. Lord Jesus come into my heart and fill me with your presence. Thank you for accepting me, thank you for saving me. Give me the grace and the strength to serve you all the days of my life. Amen.'"

With tears of joy running down my face, I knelt there at that altar and threw my hands in the air and surrendered everything to my Lord. I'd never felt so free, so accepted and so loved in all my life. This is what I'd been searching for all of my life.

I could hear the Pastor praying with someone else at the altar. Uncle Carlos had followed behind me and had repented of his sins and asked the Lord to restore the relationship that he had strayed from. I could see Aunt Shirl with her hand raised praising the Lord with tears running down her face. Tonia, Terrance and Anna were also crying and comforting one another.

I knew the joy that flooded my soul that moment, not only for myself but for my Uncle Carlos. We embraced in a hug in a confirmation that we not only were related in a natural family, but we were now brothers...brothers in Christ. I noticed a beam of sunlight glistening through the stained glass window shining brightly on the cross behind the pulpit. What a sweet confirmation from the lord. Yes Lord I thought, "It is finished."

As I turned to face the congregation Aunt Carrol Jean stood behind me with her arms open wide to embrace me. Sobbing through the tears she said, "I forgive you Ryan." We held each other for a moment, crying in each other's arms.

At the end of the service our family walked out of that churchy totally transformed. Carlos and I had given our hearts to the Lord. We were new creatures in Christ and all of the old ways and old lifestyles were passed away. Aunt Carrol Jean had been delivered from the burden of un-forgiveness. Aunt Shirl had seen an answer to prayers she had been praying for years and Tonia, Terrance, Anna and even baby Jaeden were rejoicing and praising the Lord for the hope they saw in me. They realized if God can be there for me with my past He has certainly not forsaken or forgotten them.

The Blake family had been made whole that morning.

EPILOGUE

About two weeks had passed since I had dedicated my life to the Lord. Thanksgiving had come and gone with all the fun and fanfare of a great family reunion. Uncle Carlos and I are becoming closer. We even attend church together now. He told me that I had become like a son to him, one that he never had. He said for the first time in his life he felt like he was complete and no amount of money could buy the joy he was feeling down in his soul.

Aunt Carrol Jean became closer to me too. She apologized for being so stubborn and told me that she had a lot to learn about God's grace. She also told me that I turned out to be a fine young man and my father would be proud of me. She asked me to forgive her and told me that she was honored to call me her nephew. She even hugged me and gave me a kiss.

Whatever valley hate and un-forgiveness had manage to carve into our relationships, love was now the bridge back to the restoration of our family. We were laughing, joking and reminiscing with one another, the way that only people who truly love each other can. Aunt Carrol Jean even told Uncle Carlos it was about time he got his life together. He came back at her with a fast one and asked her, "about time you stopped wearing those wigs, ain't it?"

Speaking of time, amidst all the holiday hub-bub my Aunt Shirl gave me a beautiful gold watch, one that she had originally intended as a birthday gift for my dad, one that she never got to give him. She told me that she had forgotten about it, but had found it on the top shelf of her closet, right where she had left it six years ago. She thought that this season of my life was the perfect time for me to have it. She told me to look at the inscription on the back. It read "Time Heals all Wounds." I was overcome with emotion and grateful that this lost treasure from my father's past had now become my most prized possession.

During my Thanksgiving break from school I decided to take a ride back home to Brunswick County Virginia, and visit my parents' graves. It had been years since I was there and I needed some closure, now that I'd forsaken my life of sin and shame. Heaven decided to take the long ride with me for companionship and moral support. I glanced over at her as she dozed off. I thought she was absolutely beautiful.

As we neared the county line, we crossed over the bridge and saw the Welcome to Brunswick County sign. Things really hadn't changed that much over the years. We stopped by a florist on the way and picked up two bouquets of fresh red roses. They were always mom's favorite.

We pulled into the cemetery and found a parking place. Heaven graciously agreed to stay in the car, allowing me the grace to pour my heart out in private. I breathed a quick prayer for the Lord to give me strength. I grabbed the flowers, got out of the car and slowly walked up the sidewalk toward their graves. I spotted mom's headstone first. There were two white doves etched in the granite above her name. Dad let me help design it. I thought that since she was a bird lover that the doves would be appropriate. Someone had been there recently and left a fresh pot of daisies. I wondered who it was?

I rubbed my hand gently over the smooth granite finish and fighting the tears I said, "I bought your favorite flowers, mom. I hope you like them. I took your advice and finally met Uncle Carlos. He's not at all like dad, although they do look alike. Oh, by the way, that God Man you talked about when I was little...I finally decided to make him my personal friend. Carlos and I both did. And guess what? We even got baptized last week. Are you proud of me mom? I told Aunt Shirl you visited me in my dream. She just smiled and said to save a spot for her in the choir.

I told mom I need to say a few words to dad before I left. I told her I loved her with all my heart and gently kissed the top of her headstone. Dad's grave was right next to mom's. There were two small American flags on either side of his stone commemorating his military service.

"Dad," I said, "I stopped by to bring you and mom some fresh flowers. I hope you like them. There are a few things that I need to get off my chest. I'm not mad at you anymore. I forgive you and I hope that you have forgiven me. I finally met your twin and he told me a lot about you, things about you when you were young. We're actually working on building a pretty good relationship with each other. We're good for each other even though it's going to take some time to get used to looking at his face. He does look a lot like you, but his ways are unique to him. He rededicated his life to the Lord and we're both on the same path of redemption. I'm realizing more and more each day that even though your blood runs through my veins, I'm not at all like you. The blood of Jesus runs through my veins too, and I'm a new man. That's what makes me better than you. You tried to destroy me, but that only served to make me stronger. You tried to break me only to build me up and make me all the more wiser. I am who I am today, because I'm a redeemed son of God who did not allow you to crush my spirit."

I paused a minute. "Aunt Shirl gave me your watch, the one she never got to give you. It's really nice and will help me to manage my time better, something I need to work on. I'm so grateful for my extended family. There's nothing like having people who love you to help you get through the ups and downs of life. I'm finally free now, Dad. Goodbye."

I was so relieved that I had come to a place of closure with my parents, especially my dad. As we exited the cemetery and drove through town we could hear the church bells chiming noon and in the distance we could hear the train rumbling through town. I had one more destination, the Post Office. I had written a letter to Dr. Grimes a few days ago and I had it with me. I intentionally didn't seal the envelope because I wanted to place a couple of rose petals in it. I know it's kind of corny, but I wanted her to know how beautiful my life had turned out, and what better way than to open a letter and smell this fragrance.

I re-read it one more time.

Dear Dr. Grimes,

It was so good to hear from you. I'm in college and working part time. I've given my life to Christ and God is working on restoring relationships in my family. I've come to terms with my past and am hopeful for my future. I even have girlfriend. Her name is Heaven. Yes, that's right, Heaven, and she's every bit as sweet too.

Please tell the guys you counsel that no matter what they've done or gone through there is value beyond their brokenness. With the help of God they can re-write their story. They just have to believe what the Word of God tells them about themselves. There is no time for self-pity and languishing in the past. That's not who they are. There are so many opportunities for growth and success on the other side. While they are there, keep encouraging them to take advantage of the training and counseling that's available for them to deal with the issues that plague their souls. This will set them on a course of fulfillment in life that they've never even dreamed would be possible. There's no telling what great things await them in their future.

Samuel Johnson once wrote: "The fountain of content must spring up in the mind, and he who hath so little knowledge of human nature as to seek happiness by changing anything but his own disposition, will waste his life in fruitless efforts and multiply the grief he purposes to remove."

Stay blessed, keep trusting God and never give up on your dreams of becoming a better you.

Love,

Ryan

P.S. I've enclosed a recent picture of "yours truly" for your wall of fame.

I sealed the envelope and placed it in the mailbox. I drove away from the post office and headed back to Wilmington to my home, my family and the life the Lord had given me. The time was now.

Made in the USA
Middletown, DE
13 January 2025